Scars on Sound

Alys Earl
Illustrations by Ruth Tucker

Text copyright © 2016 **Alys Earl**

Images copyright © 2015 **Ruth Tucker**

This is a work of fiction. Names, characters, places and incidents either are the product of the author's imagination or are used fictitiously and any resemblance to actual persons, living or dead, is entirely co-incidental.

Alys Earl asserts the moral right to be identified as the author of this work.

All rights reserved. This book or any portion thereof may not be reproduced or used in any manner whatsoever without the express written permission of the copyright holder, except for the use of brief quotations in a book review or critical work.

Printed in Great Britain by Lulu.com

First Printing, 2017

ISBN 978-1-326-59813-6

www.alys-earl.com

**To EE
and
to FLC**

All words are scars on sound

Contents

Between the Devil and the Deep Blue Sea	9
The Unquiet Grave	37
Nunc et in hora mortis nostrae	63
Bright as Day	97
Adapted to Human Encroachment	115
Honeymoon Suite	151
Grimm's Law	177
The Song of Bill o'Dale	189
The Maternal Line	207
Afterword	242
A Note on the Songs	248
Acknowledgements	250

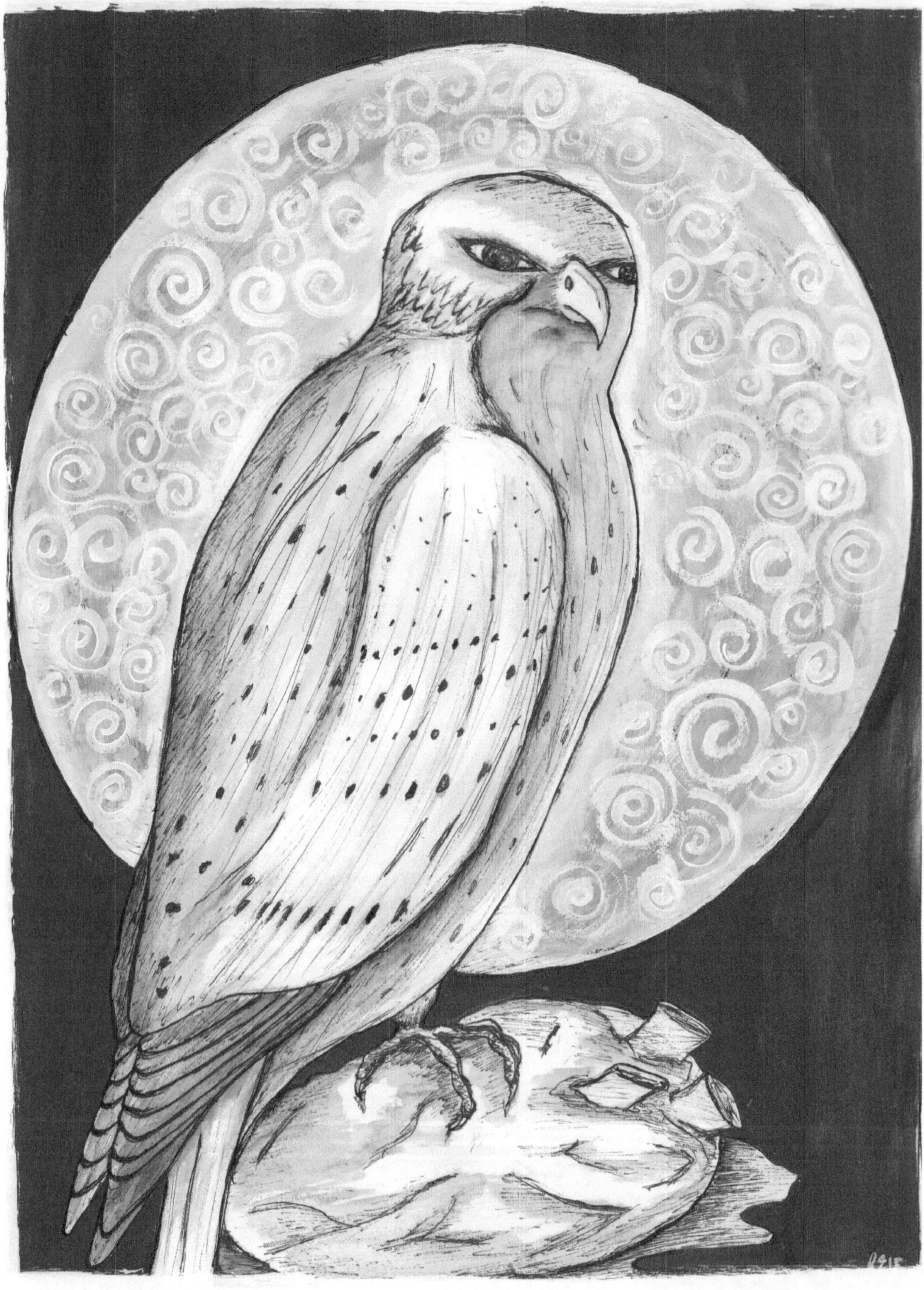

Between the Devil and the Deep Blue Sea

She made her home where she found paper tainted by the scents of tobacco, age, damp.

In school, she had lost herself in games of hide-and-seek and found the half-wild patch that ringed the school grounds, had pressed her knees into moss to watch the movement of ants, woodlice, millipedes, had ruined white school socks. There were voices there, and between the quiet breathing of the books, and in the buttery shade of a rain-drenched yew.

Her flat was small, modern, square. Her bed still held the absence of the body of a man she had believed she loved. The furniture came with the lease. She had no ornaments, no posters, no photographs of childhood. In sober clothes she seemed a text herself: magnolia inscribed with black. The only colour came from her volumes: the green, the blue, the faded red. On the way to work she would stop at bookshops, would breathe in the dry spice of them, the ghosts of words tripping on her tongue. Crackled leather edged with gilt.

Bright, cheap print of the paperbacks. Her fingers traced the spines, title after title, name after name. Her taste was for weight, texture, scent. She tapped out a private Morse upon them until she found one that called her, its jacket rough or damp-smoothed, its spine worn away. She read without discrimination, manuals of cabinet-building and romances of chivalry. Running her fingers along bookshelves seemed to take from her a fragment of soul, volume by volume, a ceaseless subtraction. Her reading was like rubbing at a rosary, like a desperate prayer.

When she was thirteen, a holiday brought her a cottage where each summer's migrating flock had left walls built of orphaned books. She forced them down half-chewed, gorging until she felt fat, ballooned with words; until she heard them in the friction of tree branches, whispered on the mutter of the sea. She refused her parents' walks and set out on her own until bare legs were tanned by rain, hair tangled with salt.

Scars on Sound

One night, her parents slept and her adolescent legs emerged, bare ankles first, from the upstairs window. Down she went, shin-scraping on the old pear tree. Footsteps through moon shadows to the beach, the draw and crash of waves. Sense crackled on the air as she walked, teasing her ears with syllables half caught, fragments falling to make a name, a name called by the night with yearning.

"Manishi," she gave it quiet form, a single human strand in the tumult of the night. About her was a presence like an echo of herself, like an answer to a cry she had not known she made. The night promised summoning. "Manishi," she spoke louder and there was driftwood under her feet, so she picked it up, waved it, threw it to the sea, "Manishi."

In the silence, nothing. Air hung, the clouded swelter of a thunderstorm. She had slept naked all that year, white sheets plastering untouched flesh. She felt like tears. Another shard of driftwood dragged across her hand until the skin sang and smarted, until the skin tore. Sand-flies made their hungry bites. Blood pooled, smearing wood and sand and stone. The presence would not answer, would not come. Her flesh was heavy, unadored. Her breasts were tiny, sore. There were words, words that she should call, but there was nothing, nothing but the crashing of the waves.

The shingle was sharp, the sea's kisses cold. Sensuality was immanent in martyred flesh. Her hands clutched skin that went at once to shivers. "Manishi," she screamed, and the rocks cast it back at her, salt stinging the rip in her hand. Out and out she waded and the brine slipped inside her like a cold lover's first touch.

Swaying waist-deep as the echoes found her, calling the name like the booming wash of surf, calling the name like her first imaginings of pillow-talk. A chord of adulthood twanged, an ache inside. Blood flowered on her thighs. The water darkened, glistening with it. A lock of hair twisted round her inner self, tugged into a true-love knot. At once, she understood. She called the name, "Manishi," and saw it as her own.

In bookshop hush, a touch of green, stained cloth. A spine worn down to stitches. A texture of waxy damp. Her fingers paused. The shelf seemed jealous, clutching the book, but she levered it out, pressed red marks into those long-ago scars.

"Just the one today?"

"Thank you. Yes."

A book of essays, a title on the fly-leaf and the editor's name. The typesetting was uneven, the press unfamiliar. In the top left-hand corner, in black fountain pen, someone had written:

> *The kestrel knows of the life of the corn*
> *as the worm the words on the stone,*
> *and so my heart knows me.*

Alone in the cocoon she had built from anonymous volumes, she ploughed through turgid, academic prose, through arguments she had seen before, arguments that cheapened on the page. The past readers stretched towards her, tangled their fingers in her hair. Not only grease marks, faded blood stains or rust spots, not hasty student pencils making essays in the margins, but that same black pen.

It nudged her, this text shade, with jokes she could not understand, with teasing clues she could never pursue. Outside, summer evening bled into grey light and she felt as though she held not paper, but hands, that she did not read but heard the whisper, *See Burke, p56,* or else, *A.C, Chapter 4.* And the others, too, whole paragraphs scratched out, the *too dangerous to consider*, the, *no, we can't be having that.* It grew thicker as the book went on, squeezing itself around true text, words piled promiscuous over one another, the incipient lilt of italic hand swaying, becoming more pronounced. On she fought, gripped by that lurking imp, wanting to ask, "Is that a 'c'? An 'o'? An 'a'?" The day faded so slowly that she looked up from black swirls and saw that she would need a lamp. Pressing fingers into strained eyes, she turned the page and saw it there, a postcard scene.

Halfway through an essay on *The Winter's Tale*, between pages that contained no breaking point. It showed a sepia fountain in a market square, the sunlight slanting to make it bright and picturesque. It was soft at the edges, yellow with age. "Market Square," it said, "Harton Harbour". It had never been sent.

She closed the book, saw how it lay: flat, unremarkable. Nothing poked out of it, no hint, no overhang. The card had been pushed in with such force that the binding had shattered, that the next four pages were loose, about to fall.

There were no annotations after that.

She held the book to her chest. The flat was as close to silent as it would come, as close to silence as the suburbs of the town would allow. The words of the verse edged in her mind, the shadow of a shadow. She lifted the volume to her lips, felt the roughness of cheap paper, cheap binding, drank in the smell of the page, and started at the ringing of the phone.

"Hello?" she said, staring at the clock, seeing it was long past ten, that her parents would never trouble her this late.

A whisper along the line, that might have been laughter, might have been a breathless kiss.

"Hello?"

But there was only a distant rushing, as of the wind, or of the sea.

That night the bedclothes were hot and heavy on bare skin. Old wounds writhed, pear tree bark and driftwood tear. Sitting up, she touched her face, felt the beginnings of wrinkles around her eyes.

Walking to work though summer busyness, through the scent of the last night's barbecues, she found the book was in her hand, clutched so that her fingers left sweat marks on green cloth. Above her, birds squabbled against church spires and she thought of the kestrel, of the life of the corn. At work she read in snatched moments, trying to force her way to the end, but the text reduced itself to lazy, silly words. The margin notes coiled black and mysterious, an invitation, a tease.

That night, at twenty to eleven, the phone rang again.

She told a woman she worked with, "I've been getting these phone calls."

"What, heavy breathers?" and, because she did not reply, her colleague said, "I used to get those. You should go ex-directory."

The phone calls came in the hours that darkness leaned. She would seize the receiver, gasping, yearning towards a voice, a personality, a whisper of sense, but there was no humanity, only the sound of sea in winter and far away.

Soon, in coffee bars, in pubs and shops, she would catch the tail of her thoughts and they would be of the words on the stone, they would be of the life of the corn. She would look at the white walls of her flat and, burned upon them, would see the shadow of that sunlit scene. At night, she would wait, wait for the ringing of the phone.

A month. A month of headaches, restlessness, a month of peering into the evening sky, or the static of her television set. Her feet no longer traipsed soft corridors of bookshops, her voice no longer lent itself to office gossiping. She would watch starlings chattering at dusk and clutch after something she could not find. On the pavement, on her way to work, she saw a chalked trail of words, dancing in a wild, looping script, *too shy upon your summer feet the tendrils bind*. The day was dry, the streets unswept, and still the words were gone when she came to walk home. That night, the phone did not wake her and she dreamt of a garden grown cruel by the light of a cold sun.

What woke her was mildew smell, was grease and dust, and she reached for the book of essays tucked beneath her sheets. Her eyes were primed, already saw that snatch of verse, but blinked back to see the same easy, mocking hand, the same faded scrawl, *For M — always mine. FLC.*

She almost let the volume fall. Her mind made busy lies that these words had always been there, that she had merely failed to see them, but the weight of the book was wrong, its cover blue, not green. *Selected Poems*, she read, and the title was slightly askew, the press was unknown. The date 1920. The author Colvin, Francis L.

Violation crawled across her as she turned pages, as the

preface blustered of "bold and shocking" poetry, that this unknown would soon be, "a leading light of modern English verse." The poems brooded, bucolic and false with their talk of the sea, of transience, of death. At times a word, a phrase would catch her, a splintered shade of something that slid into her mind, shifted there, but in her years she had read too much verse. The compulsion was gone, gone, that absence at her heart which forced her to turn pages. Half-fearful of this freedom she lay down the book, careless of how it fell. Pages fanned with a faint crack.

    Rammed into the book, so hard the spine had split, was a photograph brushed with fragments of shattered glue. The books in her flat whispered as she picked the photograph from the poems, muttered among themselves as she faced it. A young man, leaning on a gate, twenty yards from where land fell stark and severe to sea. It was newer than the book, did not have the fingermarks that smeared the pages around it. The man wore a shirt without a collar, stared out at the camera, his eyes pale and hollow in a face she knew as well as she knew her own.

Through locked chests of her memory she scrambled, thinking of teachers and lecturers, of all the men among her kin, but she found none that matched the image, no smile so knowing, no eyes so pale, found only a scattering of words that whispered in her ear, a voice young and male and sly, *Love, I find you still amid the raspberry canes.*

On the page beneath the photograph, the title, *Canes*, the lines:

> *Love, I find you still amid the raspberry canes*
> *too shy upon your summer feet*
> *the tendrils bind and I tender-hearted as summer skies...*

A shiver brushed her chest, her lips, as text unfurled its crooked lines. Bare feet and jealous thorns, white flesh scored with red lines, sun-heated stones upon a woman's back. There was violence there, and as she read she recalled long walks on hot tarmac, shoes hung by their laces, naked ankles snared by brambles' nasty thrill, lonely hands slapping restless thighs.

Only two more poems after *Canes*.

Unmarked began:

> *Thirsty on the earth,*
>
> *Even the flies disdain*
>
> *though it, too, has no breath.*

Keats, she thought as the story's bones poked through, but for this Lorenzo there was no Italian sun, no Isabella with perfumed cloths and basil pots. The weight of English skies pressed the murdered man into his grave. Briars grown fat on rotting blood guarded lips that parted in a silent prayer for rain. In the poem, there was no hope the season would end, that the low, lazy crawling of the flies would cease, that the weather could ever break.

The final poem twisted into a thrumming silence, beckoning a storm. It whispered, kissed, clutched. It promised her the heavy crash of rain, the flare of lightning over sea, but gave only sparks from skin to cloth, only hovering madness, unreality. Colvin saw the landscape through thirsty, migrained eyes. He watched from graveyard stones, from bramble stalks where fruit hung hard, bitter with drought.

Alys Earl

From standing corn, from quivering, stunted apple trees,
from the senseless reeling of the kites and hawks.

Evasion's futile welter crumbles,
One heart of blood-soaked clay within.
Forget-me-knot
bind him to your bed,
A curl of hair, a smudge of gallows fat,
You, I mark to bind me to the earth.
The kestrel knows of the life of the corn,
as the worm the words on the stone,
and so my heart knows me.

She sat, rough paper under fingertips, the final pages blank before her. For a long time she breathed, tasting the dust of the book, feeling the glue of the spine crackle under her hands. She read the poems again, then again, and then another time. Then she realised it had grown dark, that she had not eaten, dressed or gone to work. That night, she found she could not sleep and the phone did not ring once.

Scars on Sound

In night's stillness, she could hear the scratching of a fountain pen. On what she could have sworn was the photograph's bare back, she saw the words *F. L. Colvin* flowing in the same hand, in the same faded ink. In the days that followed, when she could sleep, she dreamt of the man in the photograph become a bird of prey, she dreamt of spellbound women with dead eyes and hearts like crushed fruit. Every night she tucked the book of verse under her sheets.

Outside, it was summer. The people she called friends sunbathed or went on holidays, but in her mind it was always evening on a day when the sky was curdled with thunder's promise, where kestrels hovered in the distance and she could hear the roar of the sea.

She got postcards from Greece, from Norfolk, from Corfu, postcards from Portugal, Prague and Berlin, and she did not read a single one. The town she lived in took on the quality of those photographs, no more real than canvas slung between supports. In her flat, among books she no longer had the urge to read, she wondered if people round her ever left the set, resumed different, more authentic lives.

Another postcard, a market square in full colour, a fountain stark in the brightness of summer light. Old stone rioting with petunias, the shops shaded by striped awnings. The sky harsh, cerulean. She turned it over, already knowing, already expecting to see "Market Square, Harton Harbour", printed along the central line, already expecting it to be blank, unused, with a price pencilled in the square marked out for the stamp.

Instead, it was a cheerful "wish-you-were-here" from a colleague, her writing made lazy, loose by leisure. It told her that the weather was rainy, the tea-shop excellent and that she was glad she'd opted for a "staycation" this year, with all the irony implicit in those inverted commas. "See you soon!" it trumpeted, and then the postscript, scrawled, "BTW, bumped into FC. He says he's missing you."

An image came into her mind: a mouse, frozen with fear, awaiting the kestrel's claws.

She breathed long, shaking breaths, breathed until she was aware enough to reason, to notice that she was clutching the postcard to her lips, that she pressed the cheap card in a kiss. If her colleague meant Francis Colvin, if she knew him, then no wonder the photograph was familiar, no wonder she seemed to know snatches of his verse.

That night, she slept soundly, undisturbed by the fact that the phone did not ring.

When her colleague returned to work, she made the necessary small talk and thanked her for the postcard, and said, "I think my memory's going, but, who's FC?"

"Huh?"

"You ran into him. You said... said you ran into him."

The stare.

She knew, had already worked it out, but the words poured from her before she could check their rushing to her mouth. "FC. Your card, it says, FC. 'PS, bumped into FC, he says he's missing you.'"

And now the bitten lip, the realising smile, the moment's hope. "Nah, you nearly had me there. You crack me up."

"But you... you went to Harton Harbour."

"No. I went to Sheringham. You're thinking of someone else." The pause, the gleam of worry. "Are you...?"

"Yeah. Sorry. My mistake. I'm fine."

She shuffled through the postcards until she found the one of the picturesque Norfolk coast. The message was the same, black ink and looping hand, dot for dot, smudge for smudge, missing only the postscript. She smelled it and it was all plastic finish of photograph, wood pulp. The other, faint, so faint, had a touch of old paper, old ink. Her colleague used ballpoint. The card from Harton Harbour was in black fountain pen.

She dreamt she was a child, a child who stood by a tumbledown gate, a bare twenty yards from the sea. Against the gate a man leaned, whittling. When he was done, he held the figure of a girl. "I've been waiting," he said, and laughed.

Then he was beside her, wrapping a lock of her hair around his fingers, tugging it to him. It hurt, the pull of her scalp, the ache of her skin. His little knife flicked, scratched through the strands. He kissed her lightly, on the mouth.

She woke. Cold.

The maps showed Harton Harbour as a village on the Somerset coast. She called her parents as soon as she knew it would not wake them and asked if they had ever stopped there, breaking their journey to Cornwall, although though she knew that they had not. Her mother paused a moment, seemed about to confide something, but stopped. "No, they had never been there, but,

"...No. No. Nothing. Take care."

They said goodbye. She hung up.

South and west she drove, the poetry, the photograph, the postcard lying on the passenger seat. Her skin was hot, itching, her mouth crackling with thirst. There were parking bays beside the fountain. Sweat glued bare thighs to the fabric of her seat. The sky was a swelter of weight. A breeze battered flowers that began to look withered, blown. The awnings flapped, forlorn. From blank walls she sensed watching eyes.

There was a tea shop on the square, a proprietor who bustled over and told her that the kitchen was closed but they could do sandwiches, scones and cakes.

She gave the smile she hoped made her look younger than her age. In her hand the book of verse felt like a firelighter: potent, inert. A hank of hair, ragged, shorter than the others, flopped before her eyes. "I'd love a cup of tea," she said, "but what I really want is information. Local history, local personalities, that kind of thing." She paused, ready to lay on the flattery, to talk about this place being the busy heart of the village, about respected local businesswomen and pillars of the community, but her hostess was already smiling, almost twitching with gossip.

"Of course, dear, just let me serve this family." She had

motioned to the tanned holiday-makers, the children tracking fine silt across the tea shop's shining linoleum. They took their time, paying their bills, complimenting, talking loudly. Her thumb found the edge of the photograph, licking its way out from the pages of the book.

"Sorry about that, dear," the woman brought tea and smiled wider, more eager than she could bear. "So, what is it you've come seeking?"

Her breath refused to travel the distance between her chest and her throat, "I'm kind of researching," she said, "for university."

Sternness flickered through the smile, like lightning.

"Um, I'm a research assistant, you see, and, well, we're looking to put together a... a biography."

A slight hardening at the edges. Light flashing from the woman's glasses.

"I mean, your village, Harton Harbour it was... This is where... We're putting out a new edition."

Facing basilisk hostility she stumbled in her lies, "Colvin," she said, "I'm asking about Francis Colvin."

"I see."

"Do you know him?" She grappled after her persona, "I mean,"

"We all know him."

In the silence, the overstuffed twee of the tearoom seemed to blanch, become characterless, grey. "Is that him?" She held out the photograph.

The woman kept her hands folded in her lap. "Yes. That's him."

"Is he...? Where can I find him?"

And there was a break in the woman's steel, a loosening of the tight-set lips. A look of something, sadness, maybe. Pity. Even fear.

"Please."

"He's been dead for twenty years."

"Is there a grave I could…?"

"No. Nothing like that."

She put the photograph back into the book and stood, leaving her tea, clouded amber and untouched. As she walked past the proprietor, it looked as though the woman were about to take her hand, about to speak, and for a moment, their eyes met.

And they both looked away.

The streets were echoes of streets she had walked before. The sky was lowering, whipping spittle-flecks of rain against her face. When she did see locals, they would not stop to talk, as though they feared the weather turning foul, as though they had been warned. Those few that she could buttonhole told her nothing new; yes, it was Colvin, no, there was no grave. And none of them would touch the photograph.

In the churchyard was the Colvin family tomb, but the latest names were Lucas R, rector of this parish, and his wife

Jane. Both deaths had happened within days, had happened in 1921. The weak daylight yielded a sunset: pallid, unhappy. The birds were silent but for the occasional, frightened trill. She shivered, feeling the fading light, the cloud-peaks like whipped cream. Against the sky, the stone glowed like a wound, and she recalled the tales of King Arthur from a book whose spine had crackled away, of how so many Saxons had been slain that the stone and the soil beneath them had been stained a bloody red. When the vicar walked up the path towards her, he seemed a decoupage figure, harmless and ornamental, pasted on to an older, crueller land.

"Were you hoping to see inside the church?"

She shook her head, the fine mist of rain beginning to lay her hair flat against her skull. "I'm looking for Francis Colvin."

"Oh," he said, "bad business that. Long before my time here, of course. Best forgotten."

"What's best forgotten?"

But he only shook his head. "You'd have to ask Mrs Gower, at the tea room. She's the one with all the local history. She'll be open tomorrow, at ten. She makes a lovely Victoria sponge," and he patted his midriff, blathering, "still, it's nice to have young people visiting the village, taking an interest. They're an old family around here, the Colvins. Line of priests. Bought the old vicarage, and let it go to waste. Still. They have some lovely brasses in the church. If you come to evensong I could give you the tour."

"Yeah," she said, "of course," and she had walked until she found somewhere to sell her a bottle of wine and had sat in her car, getting drunk.

The storm blustered about her. She was too drunk to drive, too drunk to care. Clinging to the coast, she followed the hairpin weaves and jerks of country lanes. The night should have been a thick soup of gnats, moths, flitting bats. Instead, it bowed and reared again, empty in the glowing chaos of the storm. Flickers of a summer moon dappled treacherous shadows through the scraps of chasing cloud.

It would have been easy to miss the gate, for it was broken, overgrown, but she did not mistake it, nor the meadow beyond with its sudden drop to the furious sea. A house or barn loomed, swamped with ivy, briars, small trees. Her clothes rattled around her, hair whipped over her face. The leering wind beat her with wet, sweet waves of honeysuckle. "Francis," she whispered aloud, but she heard from the beach the rushing of the summer sea, the drag of shingle on the shore.

"*Manishi manishi manishi.*"

In the dark she could not see if the book were blue or green. Her heart shed years, shed words, and she felt sadness swelling with anger and freedom behind her eyes. She remembered, *"For M, always mine, FLC"* and her lips shaped the words,

> *The kestrel knows of the life of the corn*
>
> *as the worm the words on the stone*
>
> *and so my heart knows me.*

And there, caught in nature's rioting, she clutched the book tight in scarred hands.

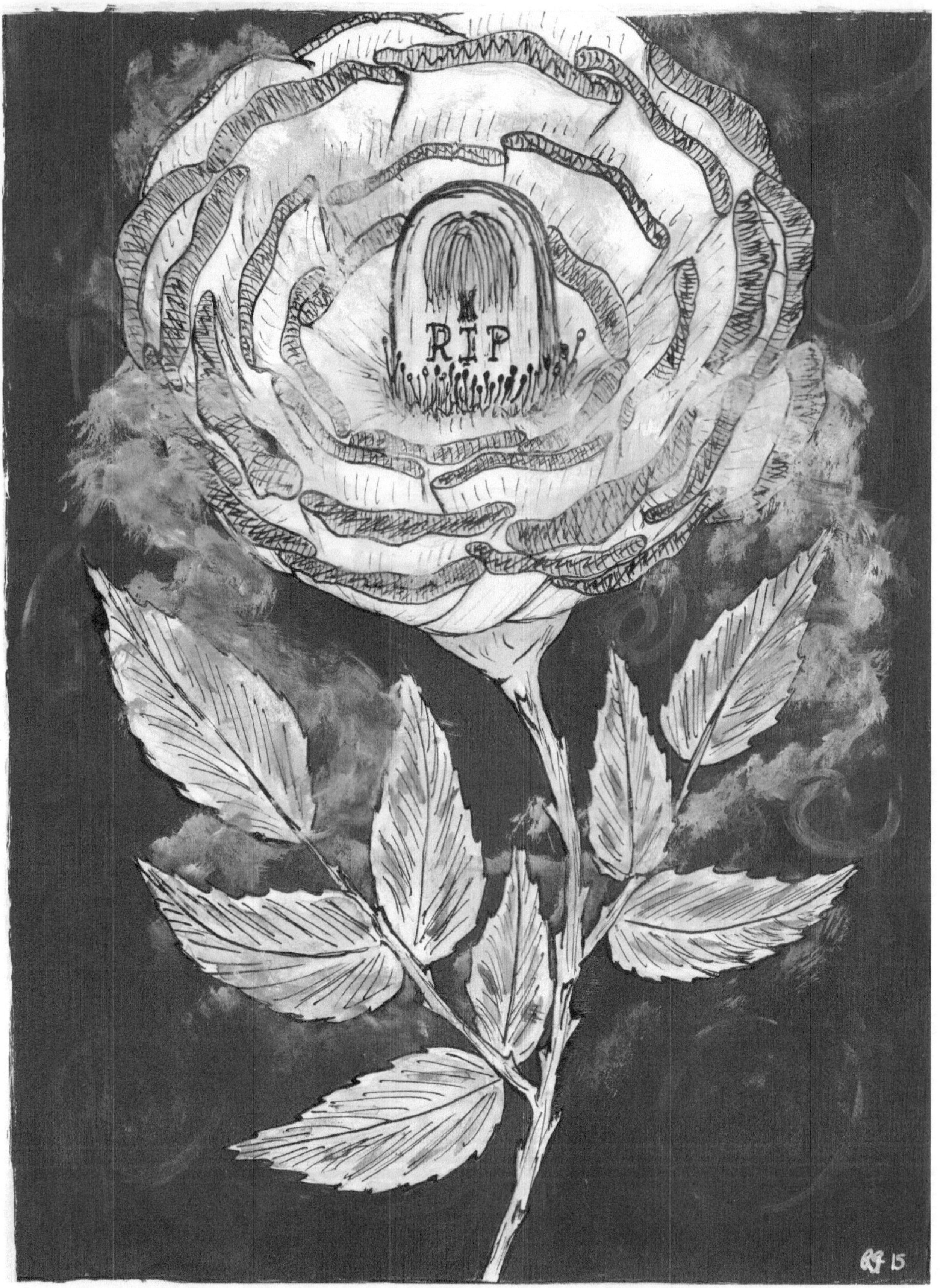
RIP
GJ 15

The Unquiet Grave

The wind doth blow today, my love

and a few small drops of rain...

Each year, in the churchyard of St Frithestan's, roses bloom.

It is strange, the way that memory works, the way that, even in winter, the sight of those roses is clear to me: the way the petals furl, as smooth and pale as custard on the hob, brushed blushing at the tips with a crimson-lipsticked kiss. They have no scent, these roses, and scramble over the walls, a spreading knot of thorns that tangles the older graves, the graves that no one lives to clear.

It is not a sinister place, St Frithestan's, for all that it's overgrown. A snug Norman church, it cosies down in the fields outside the old village. Its graveyard would be nothing more than sandstone and yew, granite and trimmed grass, were it not for the roses, not for the thicket they build, hiding graves and walls, trimming down the area of open ground a little more each year. In winter, the stems are wires, dark against dead undergrowth, heavy with thorns. Yet they are never cut back, for every summer they bloom so beautifully.

Gillian and I lived up on the hill. There, the sprawl of mirror-image houses had swollen until it sucked all the life out of the old village. As children, we would take the bus down to the school in the valley with the rest of our pack. In summer, as the bus swung us round the corner by the church, the pale blossoms would tremble, would fall like snow.

But this was after all of that.

A proper August: the grass shredded down to lifeless crackling and sweat beading at the backs of knees despite our sandals and our summer dresses. Sunburn skimmed our shoulders, lay on our cheeks like a blush. Even the smoke seemed to feel it too much effort to do more than curl listless from tinder-dry wood, from our blunts and cigarettes. Eleven at night and still light, the sky hazy with sunglow, dust and pollen. We passed the bottle to the right and the joint to the left. From time to time, we would prod at the fire.

We simmered in nostalgia, awkward, almost superstitious. There were enough of them, that night – the walk-on parts who walked out into other lives – for us to make believe that university had not robbed us, left the pair of us behind: gap-year detritus. The way we talked and drank and sang, you'd be forgiven for thinking nothing had changed. Maybe it was easier to play along with those assumptions.

It was Gil who sang. Her back was a long stretch of temptation, two people to my left. When it came to my turn to neck the wine, I resented their spit, the way it smeared her own wet kiss upon the bottle's mouth. When she tipped her head back to sing, *"Lord Barnard's awa' to the greenwood, to hunt the fallow deer"* her hands swayed rhythm and I thought about kissing her, and I was too much of a coward to do anything of the kind. So, her tale of love and jealousy and death spilled out uninterrupted, *"He leaned the halbert on the ground, The point o't to his breast, saying, Here are three sauls gaun to heav'n, I hope they'll a' get rest."*

When she was done, the echoes would not die, only clogged the air, and the circle of us sat, captured, until someone said, "Don't you know any *happy* folk songs?"

And Gillian said, "Of course I do. I just don't like them, that's all." So she was called morbid, and she claimed romance and in the end, it came up, as it always did: Gillian's romancing, her ghost story, the way that, back when she had thought singing was what she wanted to do with her life, she had been waiting in St Frith's for choir practice and had seen a woman, then a man, go into the vestry. Of how, when the choir arrived, the pair had vanished.

Bullshit.

We had told her so at the time, and she had been told it so many times since that when it came up, she would go quiet, refuse to be drawn. I watched her face, the set of her lips, the way she drifted her eyes to the hedge that grew high around us, waiting for the argument and counter-argument to be done. But there were stories that had to be told; everybody had a story. Everybody always does. They bubble up from somewhere, their shape a pattern of clichés. And always, there is the source: my friend's uncle, my next-door-neighbour's mum. It's enough, that distance, that closeness, that it sounds reliable, although there is no way to check the claims.

I'm doing it to you now.

But then, I did not have a tale. I was supposed to fall back on my atheist's spiel, to mock and discredit and suggest reasonable doubt, but I saw the curt gesture as Gillian took the wine and cracked my knuckles against each other. In the silence, we could hear the fire.

"I believe you," someone said.

To begin with, none of us looked at Louise.

She wasn't like the rest of us, Louise, not from the estate, or even the old village. She had only been at our school because it was good one, because her parents had been willing to drive her the distance from the very edge of the catchment. She had gone to uni for just long enough to lose her boyfriend and had come crawling home to try and win him back. I didn't know her, not really, not well. She was Gil's friend.

"It was St Frithestan's, right?"

Gil nodded.

"Yeah. Then I believe you."

They were all staring at her, now. Even I was staring. She had this way about her, Louise, of shooing you away from her eyes. She did it with her hands, with her hair. That was why she was prey to bastards like Adrian.

But we haven't got to Adrian, yet, have we?

That thing she did, she was doing it then, putting her hands in front of her face, making little gestures, tugging ragged nails through her hair. That was when I remembered: at school, Louise had always taken care of her hands, worn those vile false nails with the blunt ends, the ones I could never stand myself.

"Well?" someone prompted. I can't remember who, but it wasn't me.

She did not answer.

"Go on."

"What?"

"What happened?"

"I," she took the joint from the fingers of the boy on her right and took a drag, as though forgetting she didn't really smoke. She hacked for some time, knocking hot rocks down onto her legs, almost snuffing the thing.

Gillian's spine was straight, very straight, her hair pulled back from her face into an elegant knot. I could see her hands, tense and coiled in her lap. "The old boys do say it's haunted."

Louise only shook her head, waved her hands and waited for the coughing to subside.

Drunk on the rich plum taste of cheap wine, we would not be satisfied. We had not forgotten what it was to hunt as a pack. So many times we had done this thing, so many kids whose parents had moved down from the Smoke and bought one of the big old farmhouses in the village. It was a vindication, that feeling, to harry until familiarity softened their faces, until enough time of no-one speaking a kind word softened the London from their voice. It's not just place, though; you can become a victim through any weakness, any difference.

It doesn't surprise me Louise did not take long to fold.

"Okay, December, last year. You remember, Gil? The night your car broke down? The one, the one with the snow?"

Gil nodded, the firelight shadowing lips that glinted with moisture of the wine.

I knew the reasons behind that night. Gil had spilled it out on those long evenings back when we still pretended to be friends, when we would sit in each others' rooms, talking and talking and being so careful not to touch.

It was Adrian's fault. Adrian: the year above us and self-consciously smooth. The rest of us had thought he and Louise were the real deal, all candy hearts and hand-holding, but Gil would spit his name. "He won't be satisfied," she said, "till she drops out. And even then, he'll make her beg."

Then, "Not again. She's not going back to him again."

"I'd, I mean," Louise went on, "I knew it was Gillian I was meeting, so I didn't turn up on time." Her joke was feeble, thin, drew a smile from the ones people thought were Gil's best friends. I did what I could to keep my poker face in the crowd. "She'd said St Frith's, because, well, that was where the bus could drop me, but she wasn't there, and it was late, and it started to snow."

She stopped, looked down at her hands, at the earth packed beneath her feet in my parents' garden. For a moment, I felt a chill, like the sun coming up, like the turn of the tide.

"It's odd, when it snows," she said, "It's like, when you're a kid, it's like magic, and you... but there, in the churchyard, in the dark, it was... I'm sorry," she said, "I'm getting ahead of myself."

In my lap, my hands worked knots, wanting to wrap my arms around Gil and whisper, "I believe you, love," even though I did not. But Gil stared at Louise, calm and rapt.

"I was cold. I mean, it was after, you know, so I wasn't wearing much, was trying to feel sexy. God. Stupid. It was really, really cold. There'd been a frost before the snow had blown over and the wind was making that weird, moaning noise in the telegraph wires all down Cook Street. I waited and after a bit I tried calling Gil, but you know what it's like in the village with reception, so I wasn't surprised I didn't get through. There wasn't going to be a bus for another hour or so.

"Actually, my bus was the last one to get through that night. I just didn't know that right then." As she spoke, she looked into the fire, the way it painted itself onto the darkness, mesmerising, "So, there I was, standing in the dark and the snow. It just, it just kept on falling.

"I was watching it blanking out the landscape, the tombs, the church. It takes us back, snow. What I mean is, it's like a race memory, it strips everything back, way back until,

until the years don't mean anything. And it falls with a sound that's so soft and so, so total. It fell on those roses, making the stems long, white lines against the dark. I," she shook her head, the dream tone she had been rocking with snapping back. Her hands fended us off, pushed us away, "I suppose I must have been in a right old state, eh? What, maybe half an hour out there, shaking with the cold and, well, my word probably isn't good for much, but...

"I'd been watching the snow fall. It was swirling, circling like some kind of crazy bees, thronging and swarming until the sky just became this, this crawling mass of them, right up, right into, into heaven, I suppose. I'd been watching it for, Christ. I don't even know. I had my phone with me, but it didn't occur to me to check the time. There was no traffic on the street and the snow was so thick I couldn't see the lights from the houses any more. It was... When the white-out gets like that, your eyes hurt and everything goes flat, like you're on the set from a film after the actors have all gone home.

"Only cold.

"So cold. I felt rubbery with it, my bones aching, deep in the joints. I, after a while, I started seeing stuff. It felt like someone, something, was watching me. The church bells, they struck eight, which I know is when they normally stop and I...

"It felt as if I knew exactly what I had to do and, I mean, it wasn't, it wasn't really like that because I didn't do anything sensible – walk back to the village, or find a phone box or, but what I did was shelter in that little, erm, what do you call it? The lychgate?"

Gil nodded. She had twined her own fingers into the grass, was pulling at it, pulling it from the ground with the green, crunching sound of a horse eating. That's the noise I hear when I think of that night, that crunch, crunch of severed blades, and I taste wine, and I smell woodsmoke.

The roses, though, are clearer.

"Yeah, if I got to the lychgate then, then everything

would be all right because there's this little bench in there and...

"Anyway, it was the worst thing I could have done. Sure, I was out of the snow, but what I needed to be doing was moving and instead, I was curled up. I started shaking, not shivering, shaking as though... My jaw it was, it was hanging loose and it was throwing my teeth together like drums or," the laugh she made was strangled, desperate, "castanets. Whatever sense I'd thought stuff was making, it stopped. It just...

"Jesus. It's stupid, this. I mean, I know the village, I know St Frith's, I should just have... But it doesn't work like that. The muscles in my legs felt like clenched fists. I couldn't get them to move. I was thinking about walking up the path, of sheltering in the church but, it seemed to go on forever, that emptiness. The snow had taken it all away. All I could make out were those rose stems, white lines on black. The rest of it? Gone.

"I tried, though. Shambling to the church. Being that

cold it makes, it makes your *organs* hurt. You hunch up like, like you've been shot or something. Anyway, maybe there was a puddle on the path that had frozen or, maybe I'd gone off the path altogether but, something tripped me. I hit the ground hard. Lying there, with the wind knocked from me, I just didn't see the point of getting up, of ever moving again."

Louise reached forward, as though she wanted to touch the fire, but at the last moment, she pulled her hand away, took the bottle from the lad sitting next to her. She cradled it in her hands as she spoke. "They say that's how you do it, you know? If you want to...

"It doesn't hurt. It doesn't feel cold, close up. I just lay there, shaking like anything and my body felt like it was singing. The snow... the snow was still falling.

"Then, then there was a hand helping me to my feet, this dark shape was pulling me up. I went down again, right off. At, at the hospital they told me I'd sprained my ankle, so it's not a surprise, really. I'd, I'd cut my leg pretty badly, too. It hurt so much. I wanted, I just wanted him to let me drop, let me lie there, in the snow. But he wouldn't.

"Warm. He was warm. Like I'd stepped round a corner out of a gale, that kind of warm. He put his arm around me and he took my weight and somehow, I, *we*, we made it to the church porch. He more or less had to lift me up the steps. Then he opened the door and helped me inside and —"

"But, don't they —?"

"Shhh."

"I mean," Louise's eyes flickered to each side, "he didn't turn the lights on. I didn't think about it right then, I couldn't. But later, I remembered that the security light hadn't come on, either, and I wondered, afterwards, if it was a power-cut." She stopped. For a long while, she stopped.

Gil's hands were still tearing the grass, scattering hard clumps of soil, and she was leaning right forward, her hair lit auburn by the fire, her lips parted, wet, the way they were when she wanted a kiss. But it was not me that she was leaning towards. I stared at the embers until the crawling pattern of orange heat and ash made my eyes swim in bursts of yellow, streaks of red.

"We just stood there, in the church for a bit. He had his arms around me, I, I would have hit the floor if he hadn't. Everything felt weird. Like, you know when you have a fever? Like that. He kept talking. His voice was low and quiet, and he asked me what I was doing, hanging round the graveyard dressed like, dressed like I was trying to die. I tried to tell him about how I'd been caught by the snow but I was shaking so badly I couldn't make the words. He said I'd *perish* from the cold if we didn't do something. His accent, his words, they were very, very rustic, you know? He said if I stayed in sopping things I'd catch my death and then he turned his back and told me to, well," she gave a short, false laugh, "He, he had to help me, in the end. My fingers were useless, I, I couldn't even manage the buttons on my jacket. He did the jacket and the fly of my skirt and, well, my tights were wrecked and he got me out of those, too. It, my skin, even in the dark, it looked mottled, blue. I couldn't really even feel the fabric as he slid it off me.

"He had this coat. You know like a greatcoat? One of those, and he gave it to me. He, he had to do the buttons on that, too. It was too big, miles too big, and heavy and, wrapped in it, I felt warm in a way I thought I'd never feel again. It smelt, I remember that, it smelt of earth and old tobacco and," she paused, "foxes, a little bit.

"His face, though. I can remember this stuff, but his face...? He wore this flatcap and, and he must have been tall because, well, the coat and, but when I try to think about what he looked like, I, sorry," her hands were doing it again, shooing us away, "sorry. Where, where was I?

"The coat. Yes. I was so tired, I just wanted to curl up on a pew, just wanted to sleep, but he told me I had to keep moving or I was finished, so he held me close and got me to my feet. I nearly screamed, my ankle hurt so badly, but he kept me talking in that low, calm voice, as he walked me round the church. I don't... I don't remember what he said. I don't even know what I said to him," she said it like a challenge, like something we would try to deny, "but we kept going. As I got warmer, my leg started to bleed. Whatever I'd hit had taken a chunk out of it, and it was running down my legs and...

"He got me to sit down, and took off his waistcoat and his shirt. He tore off one of his shirt sleeves, told me he'd have to tie it tight to stop the blood. Told me to, to say if he was hurting me, but he was very, I mean his touch was gentle. I knew he wouldn't hurt me. There was this scar on his chest, a circle shape. White and smooth and," she laughed, suddenly, "This bit is so clear. It must have been the blood. Blood always brings you back to yourself.

"Anyway, after that things get hazy. I remember feeling dizzy. We sat there, talking, and him in his shirtsleeves," another laugh, but this time it was odd, private. Almost lewd. "Shirtsleeve. I remember asking him if he wasn't cold. He just shrugged and, and his face, I wish I could remember his face. I know I saw it. I must have seen it then, or at least when…

"I had dreams that night," she said, "wild, crazy dreams, and it's all mixed up with that. It seemed like we talked, for hours, you know? We, I think maybe, maybe I kissed him. He said not to, but I could have sworn we," Then her voice changed like a flame snapping to ash, and instead, there was

Louise, her skin incandescent, as though something inside it burnt with a fever intensity.

"Hypothermia, I'll bet," she said, and she sounded like me, "Last thing I remember was a sound, loud, so loud it made me jump, made me scream. Later, I told myself it was just the bells ringing, but I knew that they'd already struck eight.

"Next thing I know, I was fully dressed, on a bed of prayer cushions, in the vestry. The carpet had been pulled over me and my leg, it, it wasn't bandaged any more. What had woken me had been the sound of a key, turning in the door. It was one of those ladies, you know? She was coming to spruce the church up for Christmas. She seemed all ready to call the police, asking how in God's name I'd got in and then... then she saw the state of my knee and, my face, because dear God, my make-up was all over my face...

"But they're dauntless, aren't they, the tweed brigade? She took me in hand, made a cup of tea and asked me what had happened.

"So, I told her how I'd been waiting for a friend, and I'd slipped on the path, and a man had helped me into the church. She said she expected that had been the vicar. So I asked if he was a young man, thirty maybe, and han- Anyway, she said, no. No, the vicar was a sight older than that and, maybe if I described him better it might have been one of his sons, but then, I told her I couldn't because, well, because of the power cut.

"That's when she told me there hadn't been a power cut, that there were only two keys to the church, and she'd closed the place herself at six. Still, she said, best not to look a gift horse in the mouth, and whoever it had been, he certainly had been a knight in shining armour. Was I sure I didn't want her to call an ambulance?

"I, I told her I was fine, and limped to the bus stop. It was one of those days that you get after it snows. Everything was clear and silent, blue and white. The church felt... different. It looked different in daylight, too – even the pews looked... Besides, I knew I'd heard her unlock the door that morning just like I knew it hadn't been locked the night before. As I walked down the path, I tried to see if I could find his footprints but it had snowed so much the only set I could see were hers." She took a long swig from the bottle.

"So what happened?"

"Passed out at the bus stop. Fortunately, the lady from the church had ignored me and called the ambulance anyway. They just about managed to get there through the snow. I spent Christmas in hospital. But they were surprised, you know, they thought my hypothermia should have been worse. When I told them about the man, about what he'd done, they said whoever it had been, he'd saved my life," she passed the bottle to her right, "and here I am, see? Clean bill of health."

"But what —?"

"So you're saying —?"

Questions. Everyone had a question, but Louise would answer none of them.

Adrian got life for what he did to Gil in the churchyard of St Frithestan's on that cold June night when the roses were cupped and closed as a secret.

I don't know why she was there, why she was with Louise. I suppose I could let that bother me.

That, at least, was the defence's line: a crime of passion, a man driven mad by his girlfriend's infidelity. Standing in the witness box, staring at Adrian's mock contrition, I felt my senses stripped down by the wild clarity of hatred and all I could see was blood spilling from Gillian's pale hands, and all I could hear was the words recorded by the arresting officer, "She's not leaving me for that dyke."

I remember how the jury looked at me: the judgement and the sympathy. The pity, that too. I was the anomaly, the remainder, the messy, loose end. "They weren't together," I said, "Him and Louise; Louise and Gil. They weren't."

I had to say it so many times.

But that was in the future, that August, the August of

Scars on Sound

Gil and my first summer, when I held her long shape in my arms and she whispered to me, "There is a ghost, you know, in St Frithestan's. I looked into it, when none of you would believe me." Her fingers made satisfied patterns on my legs, and I thrilled, listening just for the pleasure of hearing her voice, "It was in the parish newsletter, something one of the old boys remembered being told when he was a kid. It was fragmentary. No. Stop kissing me," strong hands pushed me laughing onto the bed, "you'd like it. It was horribly romantic, all jealous husbands and people getting shot in the vestry. Maybe I should dig it out. It'd turn you on." I shook my head, fingers between her legs, "Mmm. Maybe I should give it to Louise..."

But her breasts were like cream velvet tipped with nipples so red, and her whole skin blushed when she came, so I slid cold fingers into her and kissed her neck and...

And sometimes, watching the vines turn black in the evening, I think if I'd been paying more attention, she wouldn't have met with Louise that night. I think, if

I'd listened, I wouldn't have had to come out before the courtroom's condemnation and distaste. There are events that crowd people's minds, crowd out all space for subtlety, for specificity.

But Gil knew, I swear to God, Gil must have known and still she threw herself between them, still, she tried to grab the knife.

And I don't blame her.

Truly, I don't.

Perhaps, though, if they were buried in St. Frith's, there would be some symmetry to it. If the little metal urns that held their ashes were side by side, where the roses could catch them in thorny embrace, bury them in an obscurity sharper, more lasting than the snow, I feel I might understand it better. Or, if I could find that old boy's testimony, that superstition I once spent so much effort to disavow. But there is nothing. The old boys died when Gil and I were still kids, long before kissing her had ever occurred to me.

Scars on Sound

The others are gone, too. Different lives, where they have speaking parts, where they are credited. Even that night, the invisible bond that had carried us through childhood classes and bus rides to the comprehensive was stretched thin by university, by boyfriends, by jobs. Even murder couldn't bring it back, for all it threaded us once more, a fish-line cutting our hands, our souls. The others stretched against it, leaving trails transparent and bloody, binding us all back here, to me, to St Frithestan's. When we meet, caught unawares by crossing paths, we greet each other with nods, and we do not speak.

Louise lied when she told us that story, or at least, she left things unsaid. She didn't last the year, dead of some illness nobody could name. Sometimes, it seems the only one surprised by it was me.

And every year, yellow and red, the roses bloom.

Nunc et in hora mortis nostrae

Stale mist blocks out the night, the sky. Peat water, rank and black. Not a pious man, not ever, not in this line. It's the cold, that's all. It's the water and the marshes. Makes a man queasy to stare at distance like that, and the fog, the fog just makes it worse. Fear presses your bladder, squeezes through your gut like liquid shit. Lights of the monastery flicker, will-o'-the-wisps that lead you down to a peat-drowned grave.

Gold, though. The thought of gold will get you through the cloister gates.

There. Silence. See?

Well, the distant shuffling hiss of sandalled feet. Let it go. Your boots are soft, barely shushing on the stone. It's grave-cold with all this stone. On the walls, water beads. Cold as the fens. Why would anyone think that hell was flames?

None of that here, though, not even a painted harrowing. Bare and dull – you'd thought this place was rich. You dig your thumbnail into the ball of your fingers, one, then the next, then the next. Your eyes are good, in this line they have to be, but you're keeping them to the ground. Nerves. It's only nerves. Only the dark, the cold, that nothing of fog.

Chapel. Where's the chapel? Water seeps, pools on the floor. God's teeth, it's like a ruin. Like a warren, like the tunnels ants dig, lines wavering, breaking, joining again, and there's you in the middle of it, wandering aimless while the monks sense their way about, shuffling, blind and grey.

It's just nerves and you know it. The chapel. Here. Don't think about the roof, the way it seems to slide down the walls, don't think about the walls, how they tilt and lean, don't think at all. Focus on the gold.

No, not the candlesticks. The folk round here won't scruple to pink you if you've one of them stuck out of your pack. That, or sell you to the law. Who wants to go with a noose looped round their neck? And don't bother with the statues, all wood and gilt, there should be a chalice here or —

A reliquary.

S'blood. Pure gold. Nice work. Inlaid.

Now, a chalice is one thing, but —

What are you then? A fool? Sheep's bones, that's all this is. Your feet are heavy, footprints wet on the floor.

Your hands, your hands reach out and...

Burning. Your palms are burnt. And the floor shouldn't be that close. Then noise, blond wood and bustle and a cold, cold wetness, a hard, bitter smell.

Coffee.

"Shit." Hit the ground forearms first, fists closed against the pain. Sickness, sickness: ride it out. Someone leaning over you, face wide. Pale. Flat.

"My God, are you okay?"

Words. Where are the words? Rammed up in your throat, that's where, piled four stacks high and there's coffee everywhere. Burning, burning hands.

That face again. Perfume, thick and sweet. Patchouli.

"Here, sit down for a bit, okay?" Smart clothes and smile insincere. Looks like a schoolteacher. Embarrassment slaps you, but she's got her claws into your back.

"Head rush," you say, and try to catch that gap in your head, before the burning in your hands. Red, the skin is red. No pain. Not any more. "Or something." Come on, you know how to do this. Don't make eye contact. Play it down, look down. "Oh, Jesus, your coat."

"It'll wash." She doesn't even look. "You sit tight. I'll get you some water," the smile again, "and some paper towels."

Hide behind your hair. Let yourself be managed. Now your hands are starting to sting. Your coffee cup is empty, pooling on the floor. Shirt clings to your chest, sopping, and bloody good job it's a dark colour but, but, there should be something in that gap. There should be something in that bit of your brain. But your head whirls and leans and it feels like trying to read a signpost when you're spinning high.

And who the hell is that with the smart skirt and fat arse?

You know the type, though, know enough to smile as she comes back, damn, damn, damn.

"I got you another coffee, but you should drink some water first."

Thanks, mum. "Thanks." Go on, clean yourself up with the paper towel. Be a grown-up. "I'll get these."

"Don't worry," and she's smiling like a nurse about to stick a needle in your arm. This won't hurt a bit. "It wasn't your fault. Are you feeling any better?" Sugar syrup voice. Eyes too far apart. Make-up thick and without flaw.

"Fine. Yeah." Play it right. "Really, thanks, I'm fine." You want to stand but she puts a hand on your arm.

"I don't often get to play the Good Samaritan. Is there someone here with you? Someone I can get?"

Close, too close. Patchouli, face powder. The air is thick as butter in your lungs. "I'm here alone." Shit, no. Meeting friends. You're meeting friends. "Just you know. Lunch break. Work." Try smiling. Sip the water.

"This is a great café, isn't it? It's friendly, quiet." Face, words, eyes, bland. Carefully, mockingly bland.

"Until some idiot pours hot coffee on you." That's it, try being funny. Trapped. You're trapped.

"I said, don't worry about it."

Smile. Doesn't matter if it hurts. And small talk. That's what you're supposed to do. That's how it's done. "What are you reading?" The book's on the table. Some crap about angels.

"That? Oh, it's something for my course." Smiling. Still smiling. Lips a smear of pink.

"Oh." Well done. "You're a student?" Damn.

"You sound surprised."

You got the tone all wrong.

"I suppose I don't look young enough."

Out of here. Just get out of here. "No. I mean. Uh. You look professional."

"I am. I just," she tilts her head. Faked – the movement looks faked and you can't tell why, "study a lot." Her teeth are white, even, big. "And you're studying?" That voice, it doesn't move, same three notes, like an announcement, an Ansaphone.

"No."

"You look like you should still be in school." That would be irony, that would be irony if it weren't for the tone.

You should say something. You can't think of anything to say. Try again. "So what do you do? Like for a living. What do you do?"

"Me?" head tilts the other way, "I'm a psychic."

"What?"

"A psychic."

"Jesus." Shit. That wasn't meant to be aloud.

"That bothers you?" Picks up her coffee cup, smiles. Smiles and takes a sip.

"Uh, no. No." But you're reaching for your bag and she can see it.

"Don't worry. I'm used to it by now." White china. Her lips leave a greasy rim. Her hand touches your arm, "What do you do?"

Like you took a line and it's all gone wrong, your heart racing, like that's how it is, and you want to run, but you poured coffee down this woman's coat and you owe her so you sit down in your chair and your hands make a knot in the strap of your bag and you say, "I work in a shop."

"Enjoy it?"

"Not much." That isn't what you were meant to say.

"That's sad, you know?" It's like she's going to say something else, going to hit you with some pamphlet, but her fat hands wrap around the cup. Her painted nails click. Pink. They are pink, like her blouse, like her lips. "And what's your name?"

"Angela."

"Angela, hi." That smile, she never turns it off, "I'm Pauline."

"Oh."

"Oh?"

"Sorry. I thought you'd have a name like," you're starting to feel sick now, spent adrenaline twitching you like panic, "Galadriel or —"

A laugh, breathy and false like the nails, the smile, the voice, "Names can be deceptive."

"What?"

"My little joke." The head tilt again.

Choke down the coffee even though it's too hot. "I really need to go. Work." You've got time, time for a line, just a little one. No-one notices, not really, not ever.

"Are you sure?" Her hand on your hand. A sting on the scald on your palms, then cool, cool, "You look pale."

"Fine, I'm —"

"Look." Grey. Her eyes are grey. "Angela, I'm going to give you my card."

Speak. You try to speak, but your mouth is locked. No fear. No rush. No racing pulse.

"If you ever need to talk to someone just, just call me, okay?" Her fingers place it in yours. You take it and you put it in your pocket and you don't know why.

*

His feet are on the coffee table, not looking up when you come in.

Kick him. You'd kick him if you could. You say, "I'm knackered."

"Uh-huh."

"Nice day?"

He shrugs.

"You want some tea?"

"No."

Scars on Sound

"Suit yourself." Kick open the kitchen door and say...

Cover. There is no cover and the boat is gone.

You hold the reliquary low and throw yourself in mud. Under the stinking water, under the mire, all the little lives buzz and squirm. Reeds snatch at your skin. If you don't drown here, you'll freeze. Your boots are flooded, water inching its way through wool, layer by layer by layer. Your skin can feel it, rubbing closer, closer, like some crawling thing.

You've been in worse scrapes. Water against your lips, a corpse kiss, dead tongue probing, and you can hear them on the walkway, their feet, the scrape of robe on wood. Scream. You want to scream. Your bladder lets go, heat like fear along your thighs. Then the warmth is taken by the cold, the way it takes sense from fingers that still clutch the reliquary. You know, if you get home, if you make it, if you can pry it from your hands, it will have marred you. You'll have deep cuts in work-rough flesh. The hair on your arms is slick, is thick with mud. You're like a child wanting to cry.

Your lips move silent in foetid gloom, "Ave Maria, gratia plena..."

"Ouch." The light on the kettle clicks off. "Fuck."

"What now?"

"Nothing."

"Then would you shut up? Some of us are trying to work."

Put a hand to your head. No. No time for that. Put the tea bag in the mug, bring the kettle back up to the boil. Pour. Breathe. That's what you need to do, watch the water swirl dark, smell the tea. Spoon. Milk. Get it together. "Actually, not feeling so good."

"And that's my fault?" You can smell his J, green and curling. Says it helps him concentrate. Bollocks, bollocks to it.

"I need to sit down." Nowhere to do that in this kitchen. You stumble, nearly knock your forehead on the cupboard edge. That's a plea in your voice. You should never plead.

"You need to stop fucking yourself up." If there were any softness to him, you'd fall on it. "Jesus. What do you expect?"

"Glen." Your knees aren't holding you, you're crouched

on the floor, and your work trousers stink of smoke and coffee and you're drowning, there's water pressed against your lips...

"If you're sick, go to bed."

Tears.

You're crying, crying for no reason at all.

*

Memory of your daughter's face, caught in the peat smoke and last summer's sun as it comes through the gaps in the walls that you swore on St Thomas you'd repair. Her eyes are blue, blue like her mother's are blue. They'd go silver round the rims if she heard what you hear now. Two weeks, and your hands still make the shape of that damned box. Two weeks and you still hear the scratch, scratch of nails on wool, the bell tolling Compline, sound falling on water, bleak and dull. You can't go back to her. Can't go home.

Your beard's grown ragged, as cruel as the reeds round a peat lake. You can't hold the razor now, not with fingers locked in a crouch, not with hands that shake. Slice your throat, that's what you'd do. You'd do that with more ease than you could cut the hair while you still have that thing, that reliquary still in your pack.

Sheep's bones. S'death.

If you could fence it.

But they see the way you wrap it up in wool, the way your hands make old-man claws in just the shape of it. No-one's fool enough to buy it from you. Should you open it?

Sickness at the thought. Even the drink won't still it. Two weeks spent sleeping on floors, in alleyways, whipped like a vagrant from any town, and you with a weight in gold in your pack, a weight that would send you dancing on air.

You dream of hemp. You dream of the crowd under the gallows, of your last cock-stand and the piss running down your legs with your face turning black. You've felt it before, in fights, the sound of your heart become a throb, throb, throb that makes your neck thick, turns you into something heavy, something where blood tries to push its way though the skin, where your body stops being anything but a lump of meat. Every night, you feel that and every night in that last light, in that moment before the blackness comes, in the crowd, you see the cowls. You see faces that are shadows. Heads are shaking, shaking...

"Angela."

... and your throat, swollen...

"Angela."

"Huh?"

"You were screaming in your sleep."

Your mouth, it tastes of blood. "I was?"

"It's two am. Why the fuck would I be lying to you?"

"Oh." Your eyes are wet, your hands sore, curled in fists.

"Can I get some sleep now, or what?"

"Yeah. Yeah. Sure."

The last baggie is under your pillow. Your bones feel

like they'll snap from cold. Shapes on the walls, shapes that are trees blown over street lamps, that are cars sweeping the road outside and every movement has a grey hood, every sound is sandalled feet scratching stone.

Out of bed. Mirror. Razor. Out of bed.

Primed for it, you feel it already. That place in your head where the power is, you can do anything. You can turn away. You can wake up Glen. You can pin him to the bed, you can

No. No.

That would bring them into the room with you, would make the shapes swarm, the grey cowls and the faces, the faces under the cowls. *Ave Maria*, you hear the voice, the man's voice, *gratia plena, dominus tecum*. Nothing. The words mean nothing to you. His fingers scrambling, fumbling over the rosary, dropping the beads. The desperate hope this would keep him safe.

You open your fists, close them, open them again.

Maybe he's right, maybe Glen's right and you're just

Scars on Sound

sending your brain to hell with every snort.

Cold, so very cold.

You would hold him if it wouldn't make him stir, wouldn't make him snarl and turn you back to your nightmares, to your empty side of the bed.

So easy, easy just to slip away. One line. One more line is never going to hurt.

Up against the headboard, knees pulled tight, you are watching, watching the dawn.

*

Hear it as you get dressed, hear it drinking coffee that's too hot. Waiting, it's waiting to ambush you. You can hear it as you climb on to the bus, as you sit in your seat. You know it, you know the sound, but you won't let it in, and still you can hear it, on a loop in your head, hear, hear...

The splash of a small, gold box, dropped.

Not men.

Your mind is like a fingernail, the kind of fingernail that snags your sleeve, snags on cloth, scratches your face until a grey cowl pulled aside tears it straight across and you scream.

They are not men.

In the reeds you kneel and you watch the sun-bright box cloud itself in water stinking of drowned sheep. Down it goes, down to all the squirming things and now you know why there were no angels on the inlay, no saints on the filigree, why there were shapes that made your eyes bend, why you have knelt over ditches and lost the little food you have been able to force into your mouth.

The texture. The texture of their skin.

Let the water take it. Let it be buried, let it rot although gold never rots. Some peat cutter will find it, one day. The monks are still behind you, edging around, and you know that this has not saved you, that you have not escaped. No. Not so easy. Not so soon.

Scrub trees and distant moon. The sky, huge, huge. There

is no light, no warmth. It stretches wide, without prayers, without saints or gods. A bell tolls.

In your hands, your twisted hands where the wires of the inlay pressed into you, pain. White lines of it, heat screaming up your arms. Nothing there, nothing there, and the sick-cold water does not help, does not take the burning from your flesh...

Pain. Just a brush of it, pain in your hand and the bus coming to stop. There is a stiffness when you try to open your fingers all the way. Dialling on your mobile, you fumble the keys.

"Hello?"

"Uh, hi." Calm comes like lying down. Your fingers twitch, relax. "Is that Pauline?"

"Who's calling?" Easy, the words, smooth.

"It's, it's Angela."

"Angela, oh, hi." No surprise in the voice, like you call her every day, "How are things?"

"Why," but your thoughts are fuzzy now, wisps of fog chased off by the wind. "Why did you give me your card?"

The pause. You can feel your heart twitch, start back to that busy run, that quick thud-thud-thud, "It has my number on it. I don't have a mobile."

"You don't...?" No, no. That isn't what you wanted to say. "Yeah, but why did you want me to call you?"

Another pause. Stretch, stretch. Don't tap your fingers on your phone like that. "You looked lonely."

... hands burning. Like lye, like the quicklime they used on the corpses of the plague. Can't sleep for it, can't think. How many days since you lost the box? Last of your coin spent on an inn where you didn't stay past curfew. Shapes, grey shapes crowding out, moving in the shadows near the fire, palms feeling like every bone has been crushed, one, then one, then one.

Gold boxes, slipping into water.

Grey figures that are not men...

"Angela?"

"Sorry. Head rush." You almost dropped the phone. The taste in your mouth is sweet, like you're going to puke.

"Are you okay?" Warm. Her voice is warm but there is no worry in it, no haste.

"Yeah. Fine, I'm..." What's wrong with your hands? Why can't you feel your hands?

"Look, maybe we should meet?"

*

Hands tucked into armpits, numb, a tingling that is not quite pain. Grey. She is wearing grey. The pink mouth smiles, that smile that never goes away.

"Oh, Angela." Hand on your arm and your hands can uncurl, your mouth can stop jumping with each wince of something that bites like paranoia. "You're getting a lot of these head rushes, aren't you?"

"I'm..." into your seat, she places you, she holds your hands flat, between her own.

"Are you okay?" Big eyes, wide apart eyes, pushing, pushing, "Really, Angela, are you okay?"

"Why did you, really why did you...?" but the thoughts, the thoughts aren't coming.

"I was worried something like this might happen. Hmm." Like a mother, she touches the hair at the side of your face, tucks it behind your ear. "I didn't want to worry you."

"Worry me?"

"When I saw you I got a..." one of her hands is still on yours, but the other is on your shoulder. "I got a psychic distress call. I should have, oh, it's coming off you in waves." Emotion. There is no emotion in her voice.

"I don't believe in," you want her to stop holding your hand, want her to stop stroking your hair, but your lips aren't working.

"But things aren't all okay, are they?"

"What do you mean, psychic distress call?"

Head tilt, she does the head tilt, "I don't want to worry you."

Scars on Sound

"Tell me."

"It's the sign of acute spiritual danger. There are beings, Angela, beings in this world."

Pain, a sudden stab. Your hands jump.

"Spirits, some people call them," whispering, now, but still, that sing-song steadiness, "but they have other names."

Not men. In the shape of men, but they are not men.

"They don't always mean humanity well. And they are powerful," she says, "so powerful. And they can be displeased."

"What?"

"They can be vengeful."

Your mouth tries to make a sound.

"There are past lives, Angela. Some wrongs take more than one lifetime, more than one death, more than one punishment to propitiate. Some *beings* do not see the difference between the incarnation and the soul that has defiled them."

"What do you…?"

But she isn't touching you, not any more. There is clarity. You're in a café talking with some fat old bag about past lives.

"These are rather extreme examples, of course. Mostly, a psychic distress highlights far more mundane things. Frustrated talent, maybe. Or failing relationships. How are things with your boyfriend?"

"My? Glen? How do you…?"

"You told me about him." She takes your hand once more. She is warm, clammy, soft.

"I told you?"

"Of course you did. Shouldn't you be getting back to work?"

*

You did the lines to start it rushing in your veins, did them to take the edge off it, stop your hands jumping after everything, and now Glen has the bong going and the room is green with the smoke and you aren't breathing right, you aren't breathing right.

He looks at you, sees torn nails, sees teeth going yellow, sees all the shit you try to hide.

"Glen."

"Yeah?" He spits it out with the smoke, shrugs hard.

"You done?"

"Still another 'teenth in there."

Don't plead. Don't plead. Don't ever plead. "Glen. Please. Glen, will you come to bed?"

"Oh fucking hell."

"Glen —"

"What are you, coked up and horny?"

"No, I —"

"Sod it. One night. Figured we could have just one night where we didn't have a fucking melt-down."

"Fuck you," they're falling, these words, shaking from your lips. Try harder. Harder. Make him hear. "I need you to hold me. Glen, I'm —"

"You got the fear." And that sound, that disgust, "Out of it every fucking night."

"Hold me."

"Take a downer and piss off to bed."

"I…"

An end to retching in corners, to blackness slapping into memory, to screaming fear roaring up through guts to scratch the inside of your skull. An end, if there were an end.

Piss-washed alleys. City? Town? A curfew? A bell, slow tolling. Blood thick in your throat, hemp scratching your neck. No, not like that. Clothes like wax. Shit and sick and grease. You can't run, you can't run and you can't do anything but thrash like a rabbit in a snare.

The box is gone. Flesh is pig meat when it burns. You cannot pull away. The box is gone. Slipped down into water that had no more to do with God than those monks upon the fen.

Grey robes, sandalled feet...

"Christ's sakes."

"*Salve Regina, Mater misericordiæ...*"

"Get a fucking grip. Look at yourself. Christ. Open your eyes."

"*Vita, dulcedo, et spes nostra.*" Pain, your face searing with pain.

"You're hysterical. Bloody hell."

Water.

"This has to stop."

"Glen, I —"

"You nearly fucking killed yourself."

"No. Oh Christ. I had this, this —"

"I don't want to hear it. Clean yourself up, get some sugar, go to bed."

"Glen, I haven't. I only had a couple of - "

"Yeah, yeah."

"My hands, they're —"

"Pull yourself together," and tenderness slips in, "go on, get some sleep."

"But my hands are burning —"

"Just wash up. I'll clean up in here. Sleep on your side tonight, okay?"

"I'm scared."

"Sleep."

... Churches, churches but no sanctuary. Skin is chased away from every place gold touched flesh. Your hands weep, bleed.

Gold. Gold slipping into crawling water.

Dead sound water makes around it.

Splashes your lips.

Hate...

Shadows smother the night. Glen sleeps. Your hands sting, burn, throb.

No more. Please.

The floor is cold on your feet. You dial, you hear *ring, ring, ring* until her voice is with you.

"Hello?" Like she's at the café, like sleep isn't fogging her at all.

"Pauline, it's me. Angela."

"What? It's one o'clock." The same three notes, over, over, like this is no shock, like she has been waiting, waiting by the phone.

You want to cry. "I know. I'm sorry. Today. What you said. I think you might be right."

"Is something wrong?" Concern, not panic, not the horror flapping its wings in your chest.

You need the calm.

"Can I come round?"

"What's happened?"

"I think maybe I need your help."

"Of course I'll help. Can anyone drive you to —"

"I'll get a taxi."

*

Hands on your arms the minute you walk through the door. "Angela, my God, you look half dead."

"What beings?"

Head tilt, "Do you need a cup of tea?"

"What beings?"

Smile wider now, wide, white teeth. "It's okay. You're safe."

"Look at my hands."

Her lips are pink, still pink, still perfect at one in the morning. "What did you do to your hands?"

"I didn't. I'm having these —"

"Having these what, Angela?"

"Look, there's this guy and he's stolen something from these monks and they - "

"A reliquary."

A pin. A pin dipped in acid is scoring lines across your hands. They are screaming. You are screaming and Pauline is still touching your arms.

"Have you been taking any drugs?"

"These monks are hunting him and they're not human and they're..." Try and stop the tears, try and choke out some sense.

"Well, have you?"

"Bit of coke, bit of weed. Nothing —"

"And these burn marks? They're from this reliquary?"

"I —"

"Look at me, Angela."

… Darkness beneath the hoods. Powder falling, skin that bulges, eyes, horror, teeth.

A snag, there is a snag the mind can cling to, and then there is madness, madness that screams.

Last words thrown to cruel night, "Ave Maria, gratia plena…"

"Hello? Hello. Is that Glen?" *Running on, running against the darkness.*

"No. I'm sorry to disturb you. But is that Glen?"

"I'm Pauline. A friend of Angela's. She came round half an hour ago. She seemed, well, distressed."

"Yes, I know. I'm sorry to ask this, but did Angela have a drug problem?"

A familiar voice, whispering, distant.

"I think she'd taken something. It was her heart," *and in your neck, your heart is throbbing,* "I think her heart has failed. I've had to call - "

And nothing, nothing but the size of the sky.

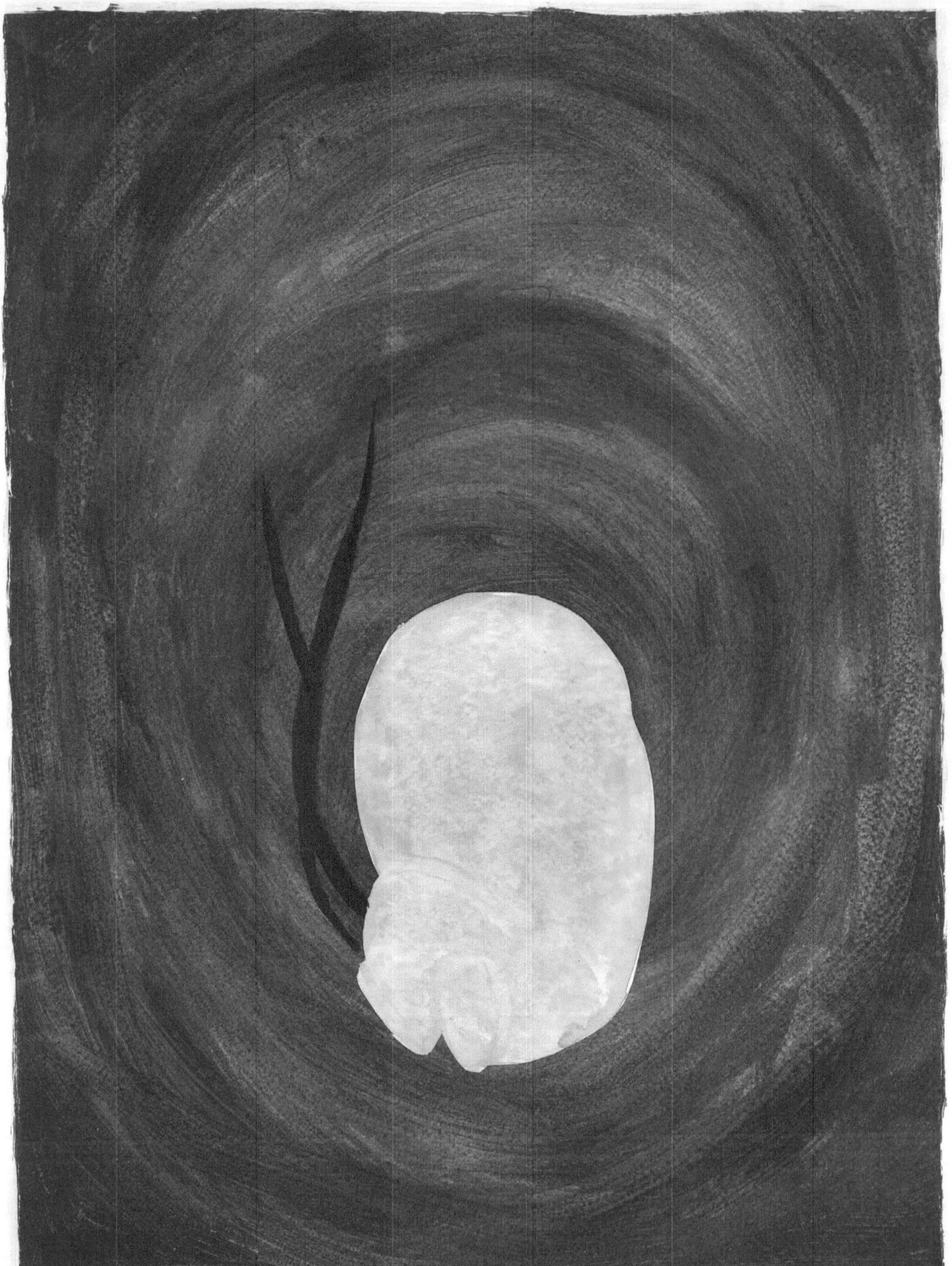

Bright as Day

They say the first nearly killed her mother being born and before the year was out she was big with the next one. I suppose a wife has little say in such things, especially one too proud to send her shilling for a box of pills.

Sickly, she was, all through that confinement, and when that weak little thing slipped into the world with a mewl as pitiful as a kitten saved from drowning, you would have thought neither of them would last the week. By the time he was a year, we knew that if a cold, a cough, a fit of fever went around, that baby would take it until his forehead felt like bubbling oil, until it seemed the fluid in his lungs would drown him outright.

It is a poor thing to wish another's life away. Still, at night, my pillow pressed fast against my ears, I wonder how it might have been had the Mistress swallowed yarrow and gin enough with both of them. Sometimes, it's better that way. Every woman knows of another with a garden full of tansy and pennyroyal. I knew half a dozen by the time this business was done.

It would have been easier on the mother, at least. Not that she died. After the boy was born, she seemed to bleed away, until any room she sat in seemed an empty place. Nothing I, nor the Master, nor any doctor we hired could say anything to bring her up and about again, to play her part and dandle her pretty children on her knee.

So I was nursemaid to them. Alike as a pair of cherubs in a church window, they were, only not so rosy. They were pale, and their hair would not take a curl, for all the efforts I put into young madam's. His was just the same, hanging straight and lank. Their parents were dark, both of them. Perhaps theirs would have darkened, as the years went by.

There was something, something pinched and sickly about those two. Oh, the girl was better than her brother for her cheeks held some blush and her eyes were not that dreadful, faded grey, but perhaps it was the house that did it to them. It was a cheerless place after the young master was born.

Scars on Sound

Before that, the Mistress had kept songbirds, you see, had loved to hear their pretty trilling. Afterwards, they starved in their cages without her so much as looking their way. Of course, the Master tried to ply her with more but when that failed, it was the maids who bore the brunt of her indisposition. I set my face to make it seem plain and kept myself out of the Master's way.

My care was for the children.

Now, I'd stood nursemaid often enough before. I know the way it is usual for a child, no more than a baby herself, to take to a new one turfing her out of her cradle. Jealousy and tantrums, that is the way it should be, rather than the way young madam would stand, watching her brother snuffle through fevered sleep as she sang her baby's nonsense to him, hour on hour. I would never have thought a child had it in her to stand so still. I did not like it. Did not like the way her fingers smoothed the bed-sheets, nor the way her mouth lisped out that babble. But the boy slept better, slept silent, when she was near.

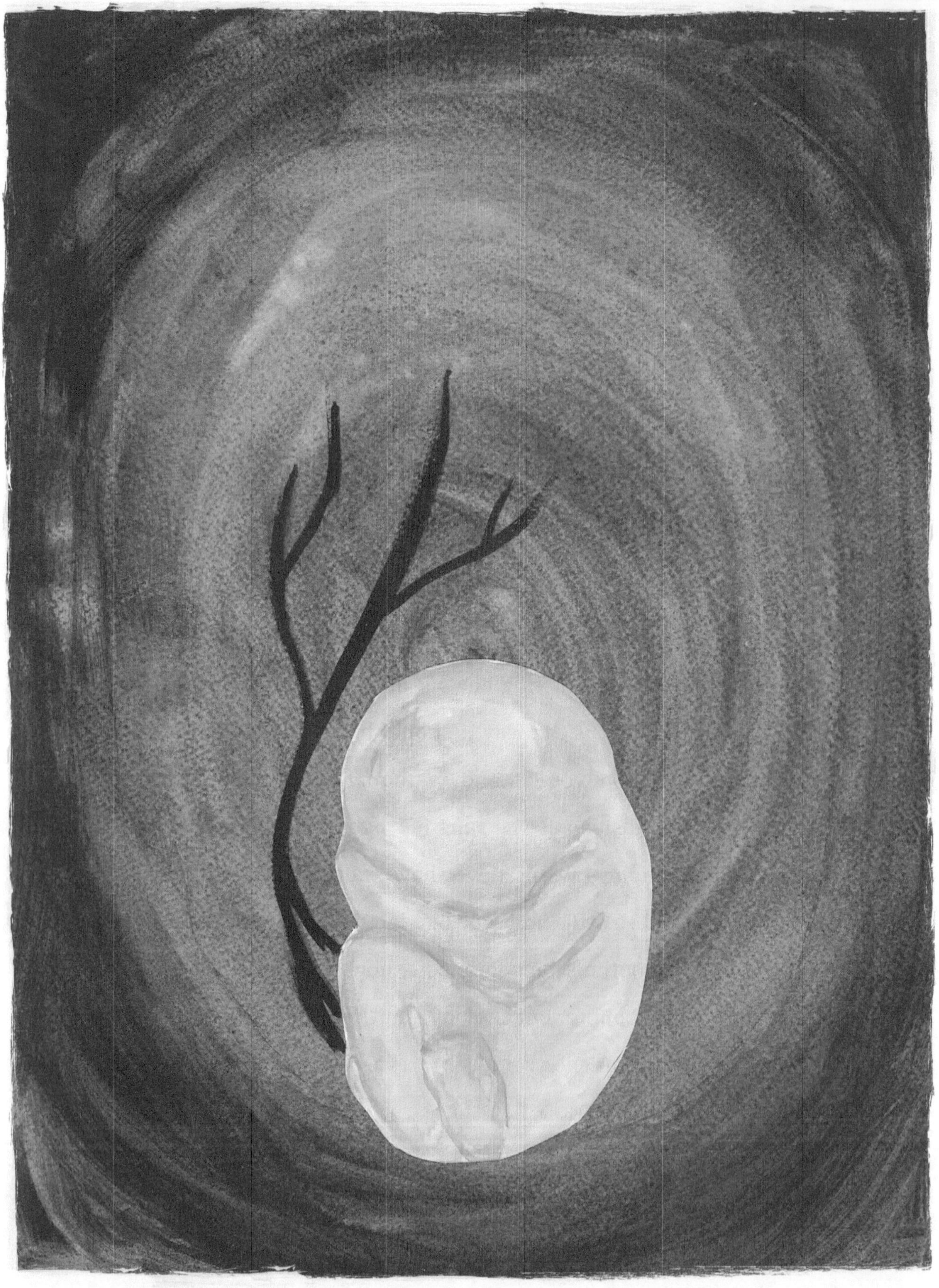

Scars on Sound

A little mother to him, that was what the others said. They said I should be grateful for it.

On the nights when he was ill, and God knows they happened often enough, I would wake from my half-doze and see her leaning against the cot bars, her nightgown no whiter than her bare little feet, than that cap of fine, pale hair. Nothing I could say or threaten would move her, not until her own mind was made up to creep back to bed.

The Master doted on them. The maids told me he had been the same about his wife. Well, we could all see the good done by his affection there. By then, the other girls were casting lots to avoid answering his ring. The Mistress did not heed it when he called her name. Who was left, then, to experience his fondness?

Those children, though. Oh, true, they were not always running and troubling me with scraped knees and cracked heads, true, they would not argue the way children do. Thin, little things, they were, but they grew, year on year. There was something in the hollows under their eyes, the unsmiling way they would stare that put me in mind of a street waif, yearning for a decent meal.

And they would not suffer you to part them. As soon as he could stutter out the odd word by way of language, they would whisper as they wandered, hands clasped, or crouched down over some business I could never get close enough to see. He would follow after her, his invalid's toddle to her more steady step. I would watch them pin butterflies to cards, or tug snails from their shells, or pass their dolls and tops forward and backward between them for quiet hours.

One day, their mother's song thrush was found spread about its cage, neat as a chicken jointed, leg and breast and wing. Poor little singer. They had not a word to say about it, and no-one had been in that room but them.

Worse business came.

When the weather was not too damp, they would take their games into the garden, a dark place since neither Mistress nor Master had the heart to reshape the topiary of the yews. A graveyard shade, that was how it felt, and they would dawdle there for hours, scratching in the dust and shed needles. I thought little enough upon it at the time.

Young Master always was a sickly one. Many nights, I stayed awake, listening to the wheezing draw of his breath, his sister's quiet songs. My chair would rock and, one night, it seemed one of the floorboards beneath it had come loose. The creak of it seemed to trouble him. Next day, when they had carried him downstairs so that the doctor might hem and haw and shake his head, I took some nails to fix it fast. As I pressed, the board came away.

That is what remains with me. They had not troubled themselves to hide it better. Yellowed and fragile, wrapped in strands of their hair, the bones were scattered, without shape.

One hand hovering, I knelt, my voice surging to my throat, ready to take the mess downstairs to the Master and tell him all the devilment his children had been cooking. That was when the door behind me opened, when I saw their starved little faces. He, the sick one, the one they said should

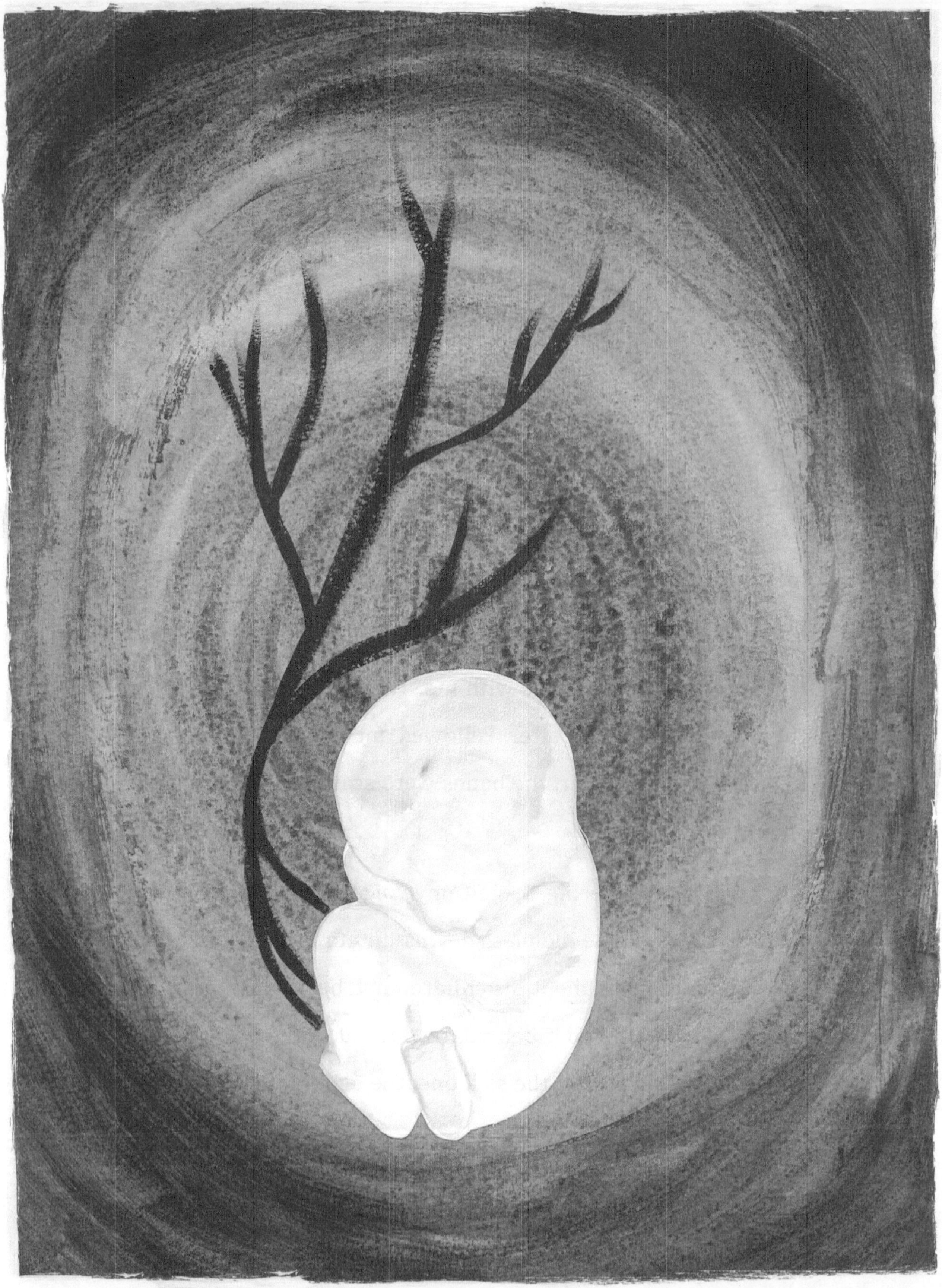

not be walking on his own, did not move. He stood, white and spiteful in his fever sweat. His sister flanked him and gave her head the tiniest of shakes.

Spare the rod, they say, and you will spoil the child. The Master would let no one hurt his babes. I nearly gave my notice, that day.

His study was a great, wide windowed room, and in it, my eyes dazzled. I had not seen, before that day, how the rest of the house sank in shadows and gloom. Seeing the sunshine in the streets, it felt as though I had spent years living with an autumn chill. It was summer. The night would scarcely have its darkness.

My hands were full of tiny, crumbling bones.

Childish curiosity, he said.

I told him what it was, that it could only be a baby's skull.

Impossible. Children collect all manner of strange things. No doubt some moles, or perhaps a fox.

I did not, did not quite dare, tell of all the maids who

had hastened away to meet some ailing aunt, how such little bundles had been seeded in the garden at night, with it being so empty, so dark and green. Instead, I asked did he not think it strange, that they should spend their days cloistered so? A brother and a sister, so very close in age...

Touching sentimentality.

And once again, there was the charge that I should have gratitude, that I should thank my stars I was not harried with quarrels, with jealousy.

That night, I woke to see young madam at my bed's foot, her eyes fixed on my face. She sang, high and terrible,

Leave your supper and leave your sleep and join with your playfellows in the street...

But they had no playfellows.

After that, there was something of mockery about them. Oh, I dressed them and I watched them play; at night I laid them in their beds, but I did not like to look them, either of them, in the face. There have been rumours since, unkind things said about my part, but I did nothing of the sort, did nothing wrong. Except, perhaps, that omission of affection, except perhaps that small neglect. Perhaps it was my unease that led the young Master to stray.

They found him in the street, curled and sleeping against the garden's high wall. The dew upon his hair glittered in the summer moon and nothing anyone could do would wake him. How he had left his bed, how he had crept past me as I lay asleep, I never asked. All I know is that when we returned him to his bed, he fell into a fever. That, at the peak of that fever, he did it once again.

We did not find him that time.

The Master took it hard, took on the look of a man struck in the stomach, his shoulders hunched and his back bowed. He would not own that the boy was dead. He made them search and search again. Below the stairs we shared a thing that was not grief. The Master stopped his forays among the maids, maids who, it seemed, had neither giggled nor gossiped for many years.

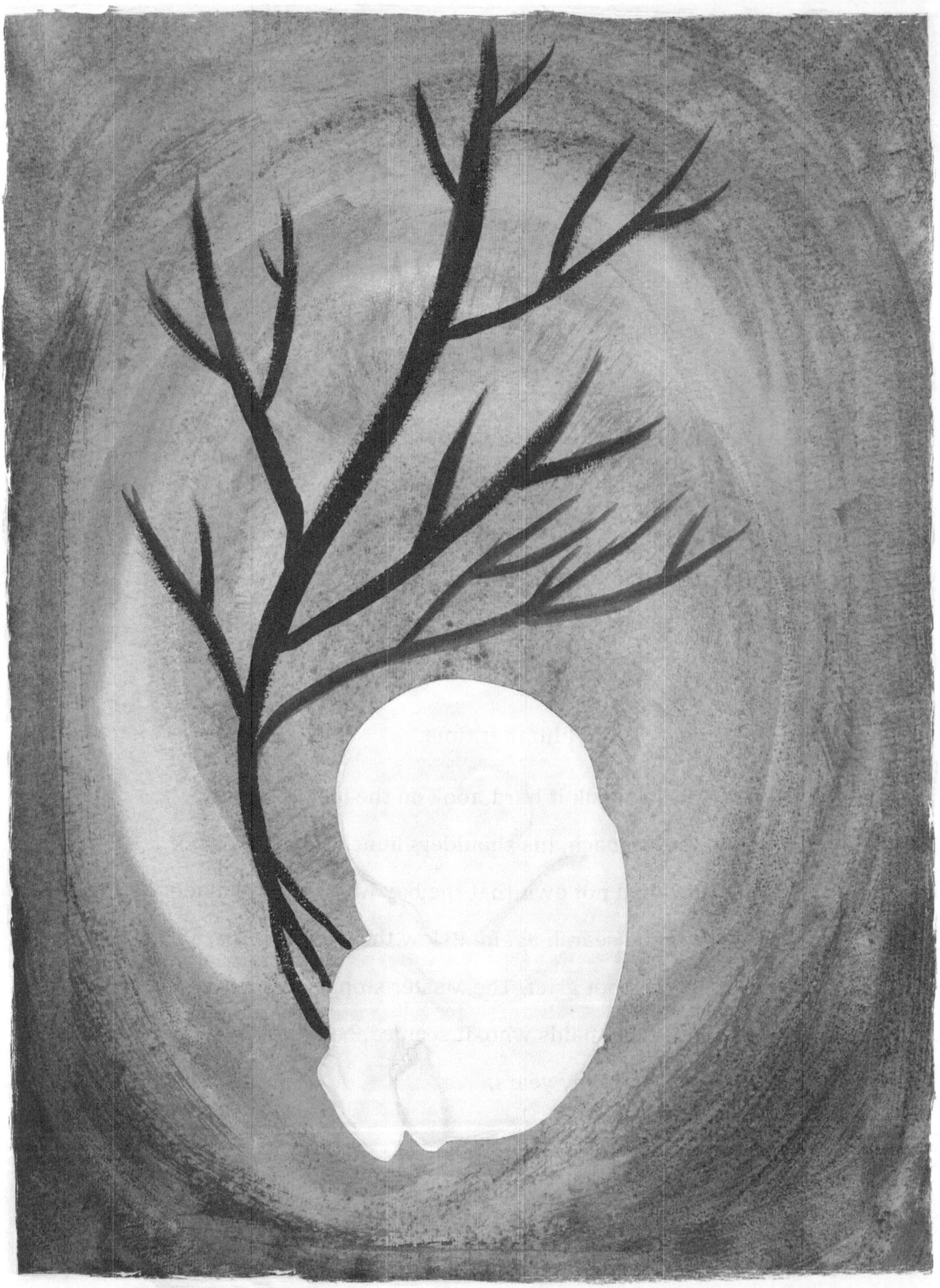

Scars on Sound

The little girl, she never shed a tear, never changed the games she played. At night she would not stay in her own bed, would stand by his as though he were not gone. When her lips moved, they did not make a sound.

We were troubled by foxes. Every morning, there would be sad little bodies, robin red-breasts, rabbits, cats, their throats all worried and torn. One afternoon, I watched two maids draw back blinds left at half-mast since the boy had gone. As the sunlight touched the room we found all the colours faded as through the fabrics, the carpets, the walls had all been soaked with bleach.

Then came the failing in young Madam's health. Her hair hung lank, her face looked smudged with ash. Her eyes bled out their blue until she was the spit of him, the vanished one, so chill and thin.

She took a fever. The doctors came but could not help. It seemed to strike us all in some regard. Our fingers grew stiff with tiredness or damp. For all that evenings remained long and bright, shortly after noon we would find the need for lamps. Every night there was any scrap of moon, young madam would be out of her bed, bare feet on the floor, singing *come with a shout, come with call*, but it was not her voice I heard, and her lips moved without sound. Far down in the street there was another smudge of figure, all glowing white.

Then one morning, the girl had gone.

I went to give my notice. As I did, I saw the shadows had crept into the Master's study like the fall of dusk. She had been gone three days, the streets and hospitals had been searched, and the quiet unease began to cut down to the bone.

What if they return? he said.

What use to say that they had gone into the darkness with their nightgowns and bare feet? What to say of the torn bodies of birds and cats on the doorstep, of the way you must press your pillow to your ears to block out the high coaxing of their song. They drew at you, like a hook through your throat. If I went to the window, they would smile with white and glowing teeth.

At night, I buried my face beneath the pillow and failed to sleep.

I dream of them, the Master said, the light in his eyes like fever, *little angels all in white. Their voices sing so clear.* His hands clutched the back of his chair until his knuckles were white. *They will come back to me.*

When they found his body, it was tired and grey, slumped out behind the garden, leant against the wall. They said it was foxes that had been at his throat. He had left his study windows swinging wide. The dew had crept in, lay thick on a carpet that had been bled white.

I should have gone then.

Were I to leave this house now, they would follow me. Besides, the world has no place for a nursemaid people whisper against, nor employment for a woman with pale grey hands and the drawn, lost eyes of age. In the darkness, I recall her gloating stare as I looked up from the skeleton they had hidden. Below the stairs, the maids are crook-backed, as

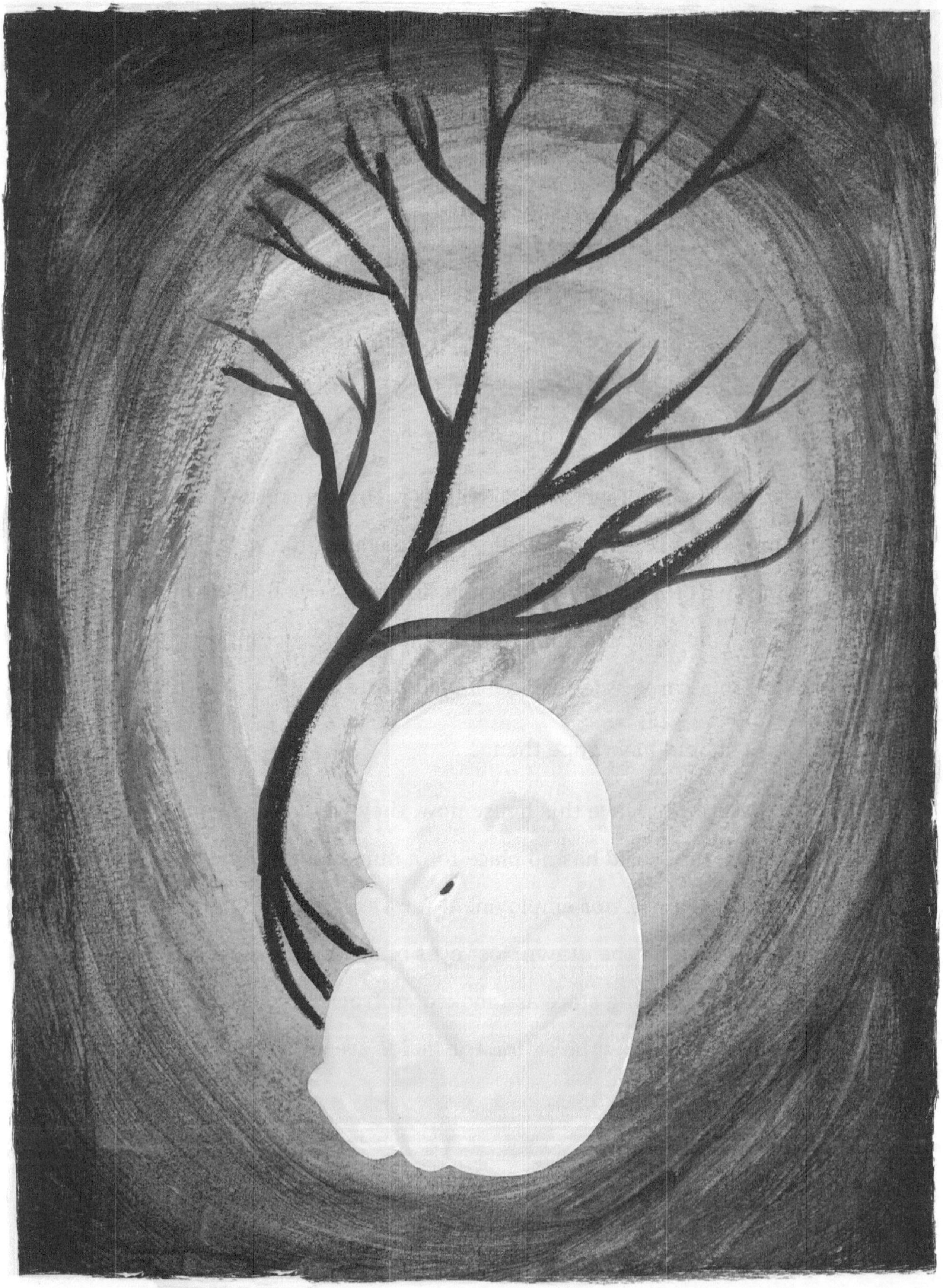

brittle and frail as the stem left when the fruit is long since rotten. The Mistress is like a lily turned to paper in its vase. Fewer of us, fewer of us every year.

This city has a plague, a plague of children lost, children strayed. Its mornings come with bodies mauled by foxes.

And sometimes you will hear singing in the night.

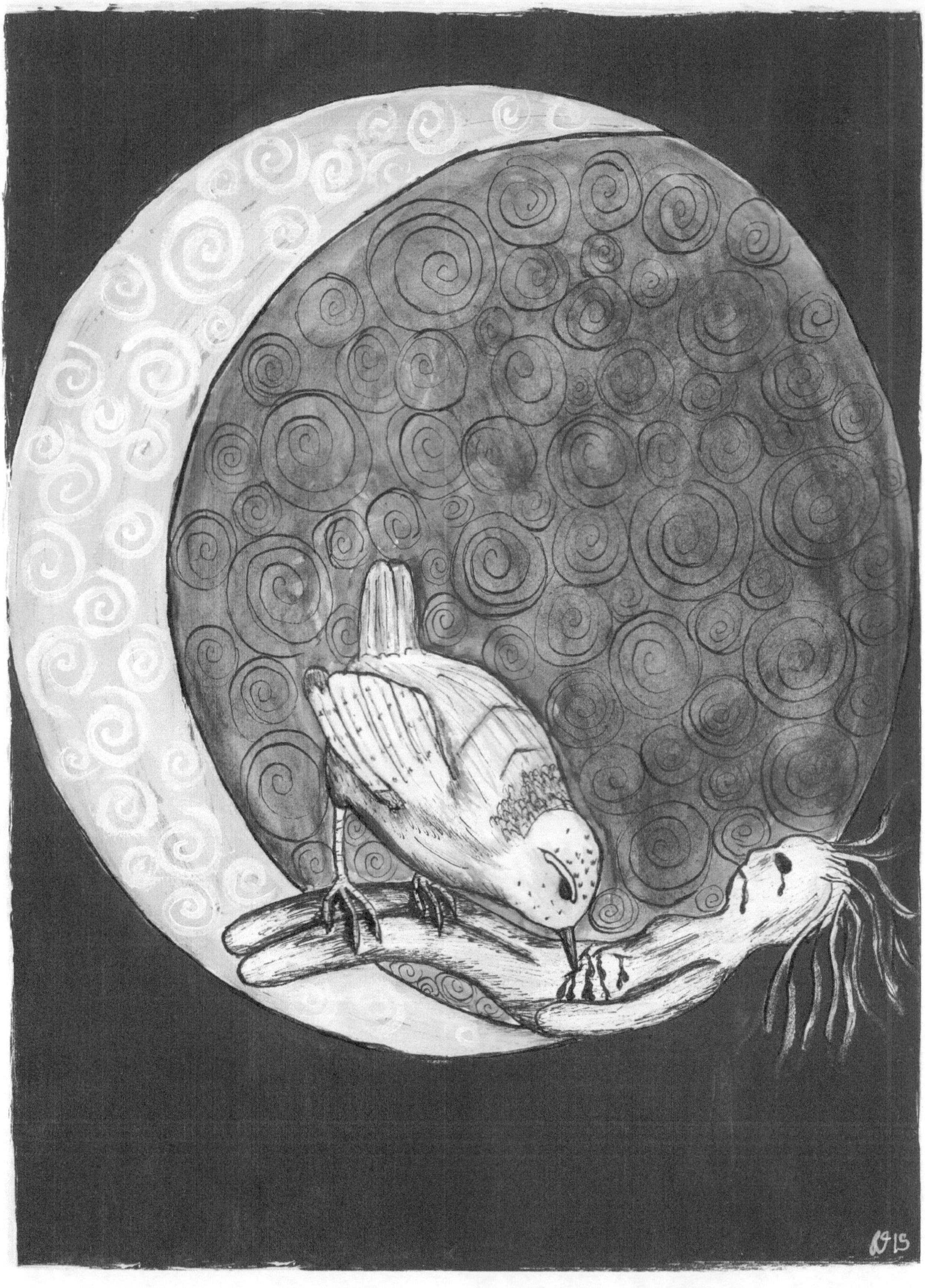

Adapted to Human Encroachment

The past will hurt you if you turn your back on it.

1919:

Francis leaned his fingers against the desk and pushed until the skin of his knuckles stretched and cracked. In the village, there was a girl who blamed him for her trouble.

He worked the wax, smoothing, scratching. His hands had such poor memory, could recall no shape but that peevish scorn. He'd be going back to Oxford soon.

He had said, "I'll take care of it."

"How can you…?" and she had looked at him. The contempt these women showed if he offered them his money.

King Arthur's Seat, that was where they'd gone. One of dozens, he had told her, the good university boy with his head full of facts. Arthur must have had a sturdy arse to spend his travels perching on such rocks.

Her hand had risen like false modesty, slipped over her teeth, her mouth, "Master Colvin, I'm shocked that you would use such words."

Coming down, the thorn had wrapped its fingers in her hair, jealous, keen to keep her on the heights, bind her sharp into the person she had been for him. His little knife had cut the strands, his thumb beneath her chin as he freed her, and she'd kissed, had shown a last scrap of wildness before the village rose around them again, before its noise covered the sound of steel parting hair. Behind them, on the tree it had hung, a flag, a wishing rag, knotted on a thorn.

On his desk lay a few tangled strands.

Sometimes the thorn was crueller with its claws, marking out a garnet string upon a woman's cheek. Then he would take it himself at night, snapping wood with index and thumb, tearing long scratches down his arms to pay. It made sense, this exchange of blood for blood and sap. The small birds brought him the hair, their little feet twitching on his windowsill at dawn, beaks busy after snails and worms.

It was a question that troubled him: how did one pay the birds?

Even now, with the haws as ripe as a stolen kiss, he put out suet and seed, but that made him too much a priest of foreign lore, too much the gentleman. These were not paupers come to beg a crust. Still, he read no insult in their darting eyes.

There. Her mouth, her eyes. Just so. So much for fine work. He moulded her breasts, a memory of lust, an indulgence savoured long ago. *No.* Make them fuller. They would be sore now, swelling for the milk. He remembered her face, pinched and sharp as dough tugged out of shape before the yeast brought it back to blandness.

Don't forget me now, he wanted to say, the tallow on his fingers slick, *oh, don't you forget.* But he did not speak, did not summon his will. His brow contracted like a watching hawk. What better reward for her than mundane oblivion? What revenge more perfect than to see her yoked to a ploughman's son? A cheap ring and two-fold ignorance, and never enough money when rent day came?

Already, in the village, they were careful with their clothes, would not pass on a jacket or a shirt but to blood kin. His father roared at this stifled charity. Everywhere that Francis walked hands tightened on billhooks and staves. The women's eyes were hard and bright, pebbles washed by sea. What boredom, this faith-deep animosity, their twitching after saints that were just land gods by another name. How dull their daughters with their milk-curd thighs, with their dishonesty.

There, now. He kneaded the hair into the poppet's head, cut a deep hole for the thing's mouth.

If you scratched them, these upstanding, Christian men, if you scratched any one of them, they all bled myth, history.

Francis Colvin pricked his finger with an iron pin, held beading blood over the poppet's mouth. She would not, not this one, and now she seemed aghast she was with child.

Come now, this will not do, this pettiness. He cleared his mind, swept the corners of these lingering, childish thoughts. He would take care of it, that was what he told her.

Scars on Sound

That was what he would do.

The pin was sharp, was still stained with his blood.

And blood would have been better than hair. They looked so sparse, that pair of strands.

Onto the poppet's mouth and nose, he breathed.

"Did he take a paring of your nails?" the girl's grandmother's voice, dirt dry around the stem of her clay pipe, "A lock of your hair?" Such future glimpses tugged at him. Inside him, there was an older man who watched, cold, astonished at how soon these people remembered the old ways.

With the pin he pricked the poppet's womb, again, again.

The tallow dimpled, stained pinkly with blood.

1921:

"Eat nothing, drink nothing he offers you."

From his hip flask the sexton swigged, the room around

them empty but for chairs, for the buffet of baked meats he had cooked up for this dearth of guests.

"And your father a man of God."

He heard the crack, crack, crack of shots as the rabbits and rats were chased from the neck of the fields. He began to laugh, and then recalled the occasion, pushing his mouth back into the frown his father had worn, the one he knew did not suit him. "I know that poetry isn't *respectable*, Gower, but —"

"You know I ain't talking 'bout yon lascivious stuff of yourn." Gower had to sound out the word, breaking it into morsels.

Francis had done the sexton's daughters, all five, as they came of age, starting with Julie, his first, right down to little Rose, who bore her babe six months into her marriage with the grocer's eldest boy. "Then what do we address? My academic career? Really Gower, there's hardly a clergyman in England not chasing after folk songs."

"And your parents not cold in their graves."

Oxford. They had sent him down a month before his finals and him all headed for a first. A priest's college. His father's fault. "How I choose to grieve, Sexton Gower, is my own affair."

"That's as may be, Master Colvin, and it's not my place, but —"

He waved his hand, *enough*. There was a herb that grew upon a traitor's grave that would cleave a man's tongue to the roof of his mouth and make him choke with words unspoken.

The sexton had known him since he was a boy.

At night, the wind on King Arthur's Seat danced brisk and busy on bare flesh, the thorn trees crowded and Saturn shone, sharp and cruel. He need no longer crawl his way through books. *Surely*, he wanted to say, *surely you do not credit these superstitions, Gower? A modern man like you?*

Grave soil clung under the sexton's nails, his skin was weathered, his mind whispering in the same drone as a bee torn apart by its hive at summer's end, as the don Francis had ignored in all the interminable seminars where he had found time to scribble verse.

No. No, that was not true.

Even in Gower there was a spark, a little touch the War had not ripped out. He could taste the sadness in the village, in the old men who went out with their guns, the women with their sickles. He was young and he was male, and did not add a year on to his age so he could join the Front. That was crime enough when he walked among the fields that lay themselves open to thistle and briar, to that great heritage of Englishmen if they would not let themselves be ruled by Flanders mud.

These people, though, remembered other ways.

He would dig into the graveyard himself, if he could. There always was a use for dead men's bones.

Too close.

His walks took him along the coast, to Watchet or to Quantoxhead, to rabbit about in yew-shaded mould, to satisfy himself with knuckles, teeth.

Scars on Sound

It was no wonder that the village talked.

Their voices came to him, half caresses on the wind whispering of a new rectory near the market square, of how the last Colvin had squandered his father's money to steal the old one from the church.

When Gower had gone he would go into his parents' room, would take the bundle from beneath their bed: the herbs, nails, wax images and all, and cast them into the sea.

He had written poems once, spun out his forms, whispered secrets to the page. He had argued, found Oxford words for things that seemed so clear. Where had it gone, that comprehending spark? He worked his will, twisted thorns in flesh, moulded tallow, sat beneath the moon, but some fragment was gone from him, some vitality.

At night, the sea whispered a name.

Even two villages over, the virgins turned their undergarments inside out, as though he would use any more than his smile, his pale, brown eyes.

When he dreamed, the wind would swoop past his wings, he would be a falcon plunging with his mate. In his dreams, there was a movement in the fields below, there was low life that wove its lovely nests and shivered at the thought of open skies.

1931:

The plough turned the fields, heavy horses shaking forward, ready for the sowing of winter wheat. The evening light was cold with that half-finished feeling of a dying year. Between the furrows he walked, hoping elf-shot would leap up to catch his sight. Blackbirds swooped, calling overhead, asking some price unspecified.

How should one pay the birds?

The boy who went behind the plough had hawk-like brows, had hands that lacked the soft gentility of Francis' own at that age, hands that were unmarked by schoolroom punishment. The soil was red, brightened by the blood they shared, but when Francis addressed him the boy bowed his head, and would not speak his father's name.

The sea's murmur was a constant tinnitus, a promise in his mind. How much of his still-living tissue bore itself on those waves? How much lay like winter wheat, scattered in the ground? The thorn trees knew, the birds.

How did one pay the birds?

The words of Scripture came into his mind, his father's thoughtless cant, *Are not five sparrows sold for two pennies? And not one of them is forgotten before God.* That voice, that loud, precise voice, that kestrel's nose, that feeling of a fist against his ear.

Laid out in the parlour, ten years ago, he had not looked smaller for the death, did not have on his face a touch of peace.

Francis Colvin kept his eyes down low, looking for the pale leaf of flint, glad his father had lived to see his family name blazoned on a book of shameless verse.

A scrap of playground rhyme, *Who killed Cock Robin?*

When the sparrows came to him, their little claws were ancient, sharp as pinpricks on scar-tissue deadened hands. The swallows had left, house martins, too, and the swifts, those dark ones who had no feet, only hooks to catch at branches, to hold themselves, trembling and black, caught between the earth and sky.

A swallow's heart, they say, cured madness. A kite to bear the coffin to its grave.

He has not seen a kite in all his life.

Red feathers stained his hands as he took the tiny heart between his finger and his thumb.

This is my body, this my blood.

From the trees, a parliament of starlings watched, their glittering indifference like applause. Somewhere, far away, a stock dove called.

1942:

He could hear the guns over the sea, defending the Bristol Channel.

Scars on Sound

There were stones on the beach marked with mineral deposit like drops of blood. Winter gusted in on gales. Leaves stained golden, ember red. Waves whispered, hard, intense, a lover's whisper on the brink of sleep. Barbed wire coiled against the cliffs. In his hands the book was light, its meaning split and shattered by the bombs.

When his call-up papers had come, he tied the paths around the old vicarage into a knot. If the military police came looking for him, all they would get was lost. The old boys in the village would give directions in good faith, along with whispers of depravity, of instability. He could feel the things they said about him landing on his tongue like a bitter kiss.

The only ones who walked the lane were the evacuees. They asked him for scrap metal, bottle tops, egged on by village children who would see their East End bones boiled up for broth. There was nothing he could give them. Most of the furniture he had burned. Urged, they shouted their slogans at his garden's disrepair, "Dig for victory!"

Sometimes, they posted white feathers beneath his door.

He could feel it, this echo of that earlier war, thrown back and twisted, amplified. *Now. Now is where it ends, that spark.*

Village girls, careless of their mothers' words, came traipsing up to see him when they couldn't find their GIs.

"I've heard all about you, Mr C."

Their loneliness assaulted him, the flirtatious desperation in their eyes. The sea called to him. Birds thrashed their wings.

He was not the nail to scratch their itch.

Still, he liked them well enough, would call them in, share up his tea. He would show them little things, small tricks, "Put this under your pillow on St Agnes' Eve." "Take this shilling to St Margaret's Well." Their eyes were fixed elsewhere, pulse of their hearts up with spitfires or fighting in Libya. Sometimes they would come with scraps of poems, with letters sent by sweethearts, letters censors have seen.

"Here. Mr C, you're a poet. What do you make of that?"

Trite, he wanted to say, *this verse is trite.* City words crowded his tongue, trying to seize a little warmth from boys who did not score their arms with thorns, boys who must face death each day. Instead, he flattered, showed idle praise, fixed the mask of youth over a face that did not betray the years within its eyes.

These girls, yes, he liked these girls, with their nylons and their poems and work-roughened hands. They were not good girls, the ones that came to him. They smiled with their red-lipsticked mouths.

"Please, Mr C." Her hands were wrapped around the cup, the china fine, the sugar rationed, rationed tea. Jean. Her name was Jean. "It's just, my dad. He'll kill me if he finds out."

Against the kitchen table, he leaned his hands, feeling skin stretch, skin crack. "I'm afraid I don't know what you mean."

Hectic. Her hair was snatched and snagged by gorse,

tangled to every hedge along the path. "Please, I... There were this boy. And in the village, they say you —"

"In the village they say a lot of things."

"I'm done for if this gets out. My Jack says, he says we'll wed when he's next on leave, but..." Her hands clutched her belly, as if she did not know they moved.

Over the table, over its solid oak, he leaned until he could smell the face powder and lavender water on her clothes. Her hair was soft as he wound it around his index finger's tip. "I am not a kind man, Jean."

She was too shocked to pull away, too scared to tell him not to do this thing. She flinched as he began to tug, as the lock of her hair was lifted, held from her face.

He thought of all the tales the birds had brought to him, of the waft of gossip soft and vitriolic on his cheek. He had become a childhood boggle.

His knife ripped its way though the strands.

"There will be a price."

Scars on Sound

Now, in the dark of his room, the pinprick on his finger stung as only a cut through thick scars could. Tallow grease clung like grime beneath his nails. His blood was in her now. His blood was in her and it would last beyond the time that whichever Free Pole's seed was scraped from her womb.

Sometimes, he'd read the girls snatches of his own verse. He was an older man, but not old enough to be safe. He should be at the Front. The shock they mouthed at his poems was not, was not quite, sincere.

"You filthy old bugger," one girl said, and then she clapped her hands against her lips, as though the words were ones he had put there.

Every morning the birds circled his room, the room where stone walls began to leak into the sky. His verse was the fancy of a younger man. Each year he saw fewer buzzards mewling in the sky. The hunt did not, nor had it ever, asked him to ride.

On the broken wall, a sparrow hopped, head cocked and questioning before she leapt, wings grey flags tattered on the sky.

Francis Colvin at forty-one. His forearms all scar, soles of his feet thick as a book's binding and burned by dust. He could sense each fallen drop of blood, each day of fast. In the distance, the shadow of a bomber listed against the sky.

What was it in his veins, now? He could feel the plough's iron blades lay furrows in his flesh, feel the percussion of wheat being sown, the softer beat of rain. He could feel the birds within him wheeling, just as he could feel every drop he gave to thorn, to dirt, to stone. Every drop that fell to waxen mouths, each spilling of seed into the village girls. Girls, yes, girls who grew thick around the waist and whose eyes dulled and whose skin began to seem like paper, crumpled, smoothed again.

His fingers found his lips, his cheeks.

There had been a dozen men who would have crowded around his meagre verse, made his talent into something it was not. In Oxford, he could have remained and traced out his life in playing language's game at a price no greater than his pen's black ink. He could have crossed the channel and bled out in foreign sand. Sometimes, he turned his books in his hands, their cloth covers cheap and worn. Some days he traced his quick scrawled words, the thoughts that took a pattern of their own and led him from Oxford, from masculinity. Ink: ink, paper, dust. Something of him was gone, something human dropped along the way, and since that day he did not age.

Or did not age as he might expect.

1943:

The sea held its secrets to its chest. He gave himself to it in the grey and autumn dawn and as the late sun listed regretful on the blackberries half-finished down the lanes. In cold waters, he leaned back, trusting body to currents that teased with revelation, with treasonous death.

Over black print, his fingers ran.

A price, there was always a price.

His garden had gone to grass as long as hay. Insects

crawled upon his legs as he read, the turn of pages accompanied by the thundering of rabbits, the scratch of moles tunnelling.

There was a path down the cliff. It beckoned to him as day failed, a steep escape, a childhood memory of barked knees, of gulls' eggs snatched and sucked, of reprieve from his father's drone of morality. The words on the page promised to unravel for him, hint at the sense beyond the day. But they had offered that as he had scrawled them, backing away behind symbols, evasions, words.

Enough.

He slapped the book down to the earth, the postcard he used as a marker forced into the spine. Always, always, there must be a price.

"'Ere, Mister. You all right?"

Up, he looked up to see scabbed knees, hair cropped, skin pale. Evacuee.

"Yes," he said. "Yes, thank you, I'm quite well."

Boots kicked towards him, scattering the grass's milky seeds. Hands with scuffed knuckles, fearless hands, seized the green cloth cover of his poetry. "This a book of spells, then?"

To take the path to the beach, he must step over the cliff's edge, must drop, trusting sand and soil and grass to hold him, to let his legs hang downwards like a falcon's tail.

Francis Colvin watched the intruder who held his verse. "I suppose you could say that."

"Said you was a wizard." The boy snorted phlegm into his mouth, spat onto the ground. "Don't believe in wizards."

Around him, the sky spun. "How fortunate for you," Francis Colvin said, and stood, and went to the cliff face.

"Oi. Where you going anyway?"

Slipping over the edge he had a mouse's view, a rabbit's view, staring up at the shadow that dropped silent from the sky. "To the beach."

"Pull the other one."

His feet scrabbled on frail holds, grey rock. His muscles

strained and ached. "Oh, not all paths are easily seen. Perhaps it is too hard a climb." He let it hang, temptation unspoken, *for you*.

"Freddy Gower says you'll boil me in a pot."

"Does he now?" But the truth of it flickered on his lips like butterflies. Freddy Gower and his soldier brother. And before them a pinprick, another drop of blood.

"'Course. Everyone knows that."

"Well, well. And what's your name?" He had reached the shingle, and calling up, the tone was easy to recall. The one he used with Oxford message boys, when he had lived another life.

"Manni," said the child, "Manni Dean."

A flicker in the day. A recognition.

"Well, Manni Dean, I swear to you I haven't boiled a child in my life," and then, for honesty, "at least, not one that wasn't dead long since."

Was it the truth that drew the boy, the macabre? Or did he feel it too?

With hands that shook defiance, the boy edged his way to the lip of grass hanging out over the edge, stark against the sky. He hesitated, on the moment of choice, and Francis Colvin called, "Manni Dean, bring me that book."

The child had barked his knee, a butterfly of blood that spread from where skin had smashed against rock. He winced as he walked, but made it seem as though he did not mind. Francis knotted scarred fingers and licked lips that had often been cut, had been swollen much and bruised, lips through which he had spoken as though they did not cause him pain. His skin throbbed like birched thighs recalled, stripped raw and sat upon.

A sinful child, that was the line.

He folded his handkerchief and laid it on the boy's knee, "Hold that there," he said, "you don't want to give it to the sea."

A shrug. "Going to show me some magic, then?"

"I thought you didn't believe in wizardry." He sat on the shoreline. The stones were wet, soaking through his trousers and the sky grew golden, became cold. He had not performed like this since his Oxford days.

"Do it anyway."

"Have you ever had your palm read, Manni Dean?"

"Ain't that what gypsies do?"

"Yes, but they ask a fee."

"And you'll do it for nothing?"

"Oh, there's always a price, Manni Dean."

"Well, I ain't got no bread."

Francis Colvin smiled and it was not paternal, was not warm in any way. "I never ask for coin," he said, and held out his hand.

After a moment the child offered his own. It was slimed by sweat, tufted with freckles and fine, auburn hair.

Inside him, something twisted, a hangman's drop, a

noose woven from sand. His own fingers were beaded with grit, slick with tallow.

"Your parents are dead, Manni Dean."

The boy flinched, "No they ain't."

"You live in Spitalfields? Along Dray Walk?"

A nod.

"Two nights ago your neighbour took a direct hit. Your mother was helping with," he prodded the lines with his fingers, forcing them to tell their tale, "her daughter. With her daughter's wedding dress."

"You're trying to scare me. I —"

He gripped the hand, hard, hard, until the boy was quiet, "Your father is in North Africa."

The grime was stark on the child's sour-milk skin.

"Missing in action, and we both know what that means."

"Liar." The voice was hate, but the eye – the eyes believed.

"Your mother has had the telegram three weeks. She was

trying to think of how to tell you. You haven't had a letter in a month."

"That pillock Gower, he told you. He told you that."

"The village brats won't come within a mile of here. You know that. This is magic, Manni Dean," he dropped the hand and smiled, "were you expecting a flash and a bang?"

"I'll get the rozzers on you." The child's face glistened with snot streaks and tears.

Francis Colvin leaned back onto the stones and stretched out his hand. "My book, please, Manni Dean. And my handkerchief."

1968:

The ivy had blocked the windows, the light. The house was dusty with it, its bitterness hiding in the air the way a throat hides a cough. Its tendrils probed cracks into the wall, knocking mortar down in thin streams, letting in the rain with the wet slap of leaves.

As a boy, he had made a collection of eggs, each blown and labelled, laid in unspun wool. If he held them now, their shells were cool, smooth, a promise broken, a life that he had robbed.

How could he repay the birds?

Dean stood in the doorway. What could he see? The house was dark. To approach it would to be to walk towards a void, to step into a square of black the width and height of a grave.

Francis Colvin leaned against the wall, his pen without ink, marking the air with idle lines, watching as Dean's foot tapped the witch-bottle, sent it on a sloshing roll into the ivy roots.

"I should leave that there." His voice was thin, still. Still a child's voice.

"You sold the book?"

"You don't even care. I remember what you did to Freddy Gower, but now, down in the village they're ill-willing you and you don't even care."

"Did you sell the book?"

"Yes, I sold it."

Lying.

Dean picked up the bottle with fingertips that were scarred. Inside it, pins rattled. The clay was poorly thrown.

Francis had found the nest in the attic where the roof had fallen through.

He felt like a hawk with a broken wing.

"In the village, they are selling every scrap of their grandfathers' land."

Dean lay the bottle on the table, shrugged.

"I haven't seen a buzzard in weeks."

"Myxomatosis," Dean's voice had never been able to shake the London from its vowels, "food chains. You taught me that."

Francis Colvin spat on the floor, "You should have sold the book."

"What is wrong with you today?"

"I'm old."

"Saw the Gower girl in the market square. You telling her that?"

"She's on the pill." He dropped each word like it was heavy, pebbles hurled into the sea.

"I'm not staying. Not if you're like this."

He stood, Francis Colvin stood. A tall man, very tall, his shirt white. "Oh, you'll stay, Manni Dean."

Dean's fingers coiled, hands turned to fists. "Don't." Behind the face that Suez had seen, the hands that had put him inside twice and all the learning he had grasped, there was still that little boy, two trails of snot running down his face and a blood-stained handkerchief on his knee.

Francis Colvin walked towards his guest, "Do you want me to read your palm again?"

"Bastard."

Between his fingers he pinched the stubbled skin at the corner of Dean's mouth just as, in his mind, his fingers found a linen thread, hair thin and soaked in blood.

"Mind your manners, Dean."

The Gower girl, Ann, had long white legs that stretched and peeped from cheesecloth skirts, that ended in feet with soles walking had made black. Her hands teased buttercups from the grass, weaving them into bangles for her wrists.

Don't, he wanted to say.

"I wrote a poem once," he said, "about a girl like you." He was not lying, or not quite.

"I know." She fought with her father every night. Like all her friends, she faked a drawl, part Yankee and part Scouse. Even beneath him, even with the thistles on her back, it was for London that she twitched. She flicked her finished cigarette into the dry grass.

Don't, he wanted to say, again.

"How do you know?" he asked, instead.

Already, her fingertips were smudged with yellow stains. "Mr Dean showed me," and she tutted, laid on the condemnation of her kind, "he's such a square."

The woodbine was blown and waved its hollow twigs against the sky. The fields were dry with harvest dust. Manni Dean had taken a camera from his car. He worked with images, always held back from matter's flesh, not feeling the rain to be the spit in his mouth, nor the grass soughing to be his hair, prickling at each shadow over the sun.

What legacy.

The girl had flowers daubed upon her cheeks.

I knew your mother, he almost said, *your grandmother.* But she leaned over and kissed him. Her lips were stale with smoke. She was a child, her bones white and half-glimpsed beneath the skin.

"You're cool, though," a whisper in his mouth, fingers tugging hair that he combed back, that was as black as it had been before she was conceived, when there had still been buzzards wheeling by the coast. "Are you really a sorcerer?"

He did not speak, feeling the pain as her grip did not release. She was as soft, as tart as June fruit eaten in late May. Her hair was a tangle, all plaits and flowers flowing down her back. He knew he was not the only man she fucked.

The breeze lifted long strands of her hair, catching on the grass tips. In the hedges, birds moved, eager for the bartering.

"Smile." The command floated to them, not quite a thing of wind, not quite the ocean's roar.

Francis Colvin stood and walked away. Manni's camera licked the day with light.

"You'll never get a shot of him," said the Gower girl, and she laughed.

"Never let a man take your name," he said, "or your image, or your blood."

"You took my blood once," said Manni Dean.

Scars on Sound

"Then isn't it a good thing you trust me?"

The girl tilted her head to one side, laid it along arms that bruised like crocuses in spring. "I'm going to be a model," she said, "in London."

There had been eggs in the nest, eggs the kestrels had left, the life in them addled, the shells thin with protection failed.

He could see inside her, see the drop of his own blood that had lain alongside her in the womb. He could reach into her mind, pluck out the dreams there and she would never know that they were gone. He could bind her to his side, the way he had bound Manni Dean.

The wind was bitter with the poison the farmers spread upon the wheat, the rabbits in their burrows red-eyed and fever dead. He could feel the land shift beneath his skin.

He had written once that his heart was unknown to him.

"The poems, Manni Dean."

Dean knelt by the Gower girl, whispering words to her,

words he could not hear, and his fingers brushed the cracking paint on her cheek, flowers falling away. When he looked up he said, "I told you, I sold them."

"They are in your car."

When his father had lived, it had been a lane to the rectory, in spring a flood, in winter mountains of hard ice waiting to be stubbed by your feet. It was tarmac now, roads slipping over the village like bonds laid while it was sleeping. When he walked along the cliff-top his feet were scratched by rabbit trails that had grown fat, scarred skins.

In the village, as their children ran down to London after lies of peace and free love, they blamed him for sour milk, for dogs grown sick and jam that would not set. Their ill wills fell on his face like stray hairs, his name invoked like sparrow claws perching on his skin. Strangers moved down from the towns but did not stay. He had grown diffuse, a bogeyman, a ghost story that faded.

The past will hurt you, if your turn you back on it.

Scars on Sound

Dean's car smelled of canvas, of petrol and sweat, but the volume of verse was damp and cold, as though it had heard tell of winter, of night.

The sun slid down the sky, brushing everything with the ghost of warmth.

Time, it was almost time.

Dean's fingers were on her arm, her eyes like blackberries snatched before a frost. There was power in the land. His little magics twisted and flexed, thermals keeping him aloft, strands of hair and drops of blood, his children unacknowledged, children with kestrels' eyes.

In the drawers of the desk where his father's sermons were scratched out, there was a linen square brown with blood, but it was not Manni Dean. It had never been Manni Dean.

Behind him, the sea whispered a name, a name he almost knew. Leaning on the gate, Francis Colvin smiled like a swooping hawk, "Manni," he said, and the camera came up to capture him.

Honeymoon Suite

They are right to say this house is haunted.

Though time has passed, the thought of him will come to me like the soft drift of muslin across floors untrodden. He is here, in the darkness. I recall his smile, the touch of his hand; memories as soft as the sheets I lay upon when the buttons of his boots pressed naked skin, when his breath came quiet in sleep.

Soft, as I have said. His spirit has other moods. There are nightmares enough to break the sleep of an eternity. You would do well to beware of love.

I was beautiful, then.

Come, you need not look away. I have been marred by life, I know it. They are my sadnesses, these scars. But then, long ago, I had not felt the touch, or scorn, or love of any man. I was as sealed as a nun: fair, rich, pure, budding like a rose of the kind you do not let harsh winds burn. The night

I met him, I did not even understand his appraisal, only felt something smoulder down my spine, something scorch my virgin skin. I turned, I recall, I turned bewildered and I saw...

Ah, the grace of him. His lips' proud set, the crawling deference of the other men. I stared, for how long I know not. I was absorbed by the movement of muscle under his skin, the swish of the room ordering itself to his liking. I stared so long I drew his gaze again, and so he came, and bowed, and took my hand.

We waltzed. That was enough to stir scandal around me, for, country girl that I was, I had no skirts of London fashion to guard me from his hips. His hand upon my waist, the awe beating in my chest and I was lost, lost. At our dance's end, I would have fallen at his feet had his arms not still constrained me. He laid his kiss upon my neck, rasp of stubble, stab of tooth, and whispered that my silence pleased him.

I sat out from the other dances. I could not think, could barely converse. The evening stretched as long as the rack, while I watched him dance, flirt, captivate. I knew, I quivered with the knowledge that this creature was no man, that he would not posture, gaseous and dull, for royal favour. I watched him, waiting for his knowing smile, his brief, ironic bow. The longer I was denied, the louder my hunger roared.

There were many that night who wooed me, thronging as bothersome as flies. I might have danced, or spoken, or surrendered in love to any of them. But there was no hope. My living heart, my soul, everything of me had been wrenched out and lay under his dominion. I have told you; you would do well to beware of love.

Even that night, there were whispers: how I had been marked out for honours denied those greater, if less fair. Already, too, rumours of my hauteur, my lack of proper deference. London was its usual stew of gossip and ill-favour and I cared not for the opinion of the crowd. What were idle, acid tongues to his eyes? What fatuous opinion to the dark whisper of his voice? Already, you see, I was his slave.

And I was a fool.

Alys Earl

That night he came to seal our contract in maiden blood. In the house my father had taken on the city's edge, I lay feverish between white sheets. From time to time, my fingers found the burn his kiss had left upon my neck and, lost to sleep, I felt its heat spread through me. When it seemed as though my body had become one strand of liquid fire, he came. I was inept in my youth, my desperation to please. His hands became stern tutors. I learnt to love his way: when to move, when to lie still, when to feel pain. I learnt when to moan, to cry, to stifle my ecstasy into silence. I learnt much, then, but never found it strange that a blow, a scratch, a bite that drew blood and made me scream should be both reprimand and reward.

His fingertips made skin ache and burn. His teeth left pale bruises on the hard flesh of my neck. My breasts, my wrist, my hips were patterned with the deep sore marks left by his rings. I became his.

He whispered to me the name of this magic to me. The words fell on virgin ears, and I made of them something

Scars on Sound

sacred, something new. Nothing in my child's foolishness could connect this with the grim duty at which my married friends would hint. It was not meant, surely, it was not known, for mortal flesh to feel this way. I struggled in my heavy skin to become fit meat for his divinity. The cool air blazed as he pinched my nipples, clawed my skin, as he made me contort and strive and pray. This terrible sweetness was a thing for gods, for Eden. It was as though agony and ecstasy were but chords, and to play them thus would make a song, one which haunted, one which compelled. So I rejoiced, and gave my life to follow the tune to its inevitable end.

I thought it a dream. When light returned, I believed my adoration had spilled over into wicked, alluring dreams. Then day revealed the marks of passion, wounds I wore like badges of pride. Each time my stays pinched some swelling bruise, each time a cut yielded a sting as keen as whiplash, I smiled to myself, the secret glowing in my flesh.

After that, he came most nights. Most mornings, I awoke drained of life and love. When he did not come, I wept until the dawn crept, eerie, over the horizon. Then, listless, I would despond in want of the nourishment of his kisses, his punishment, his seed. But I no longer begged him, no longer marked his absence with complaint. I knew what to expect, if I displeased.

Daylight, then, was painful, as was human company. To have it forced upon me made me spiteful, quarrelsome, proud. My father's eyes showed hurt when I turned my suitors away with such curtness that they came no more. But what was the hurt in my father's eyes to my beloved's glare? I was his, I swore it to him each time he permitted me to speak. The thought of giving another any fragment of regard repelled me, as devout believers repel the devil. I lived in holy terror of his punishments, his retributions. His rejection.

Of course, I regret this now.

It happened. After all, he came night by night, month by month. I woke most mornings fuck-ridden and sore, his spending dripping down my legs.

Scars on Sound

Of course it happened.

The sun's rising brought a fresh affliction; a sickness that would not pass. Soon, too, my breasts were tender, sore. My stomach began to swell. His child. It was his child that had been spawned inside me with midnight and pain, his child who stretched and grew like wheat towards the sun.

A secret beneath the silk of my shift, where his scars burnt. And I was glad. Glad.

It is hard to credit that I was so naïve.

Well, my father was not so much the fool. It was with sadness, not anger, that he demanded his changeling daughter tell him the father of her child. I would not. No doubt he suspected some eager gardener's boy, suspected me of rolling in the hay with some lad of common hire, someone with calloused hands who blew his nose upon his sleeve and had once blinded me shy with his whistles and smiles.

I sneered.

He insisted, demanded that, if I would not tell, I myself must seek out the man, must force him into marriage.

Force?

Oh, my Lord loved me to beg before him for some trifle: a kiss, a glimpse of the body he rarely let my fingers profane. But force?

One night, sore and bloody, shaking under his fists and his whip and his spurs, I had begged for gentleness. He gave me pain. Pain that scarred and burnt, divine pain that went beyond screaming and tears and consciousness until it found a single note of hopelessness and despair. Such pain. I could not, I dared not even raise the matter before him.

At first, he laughed, *A man does not marry his whore.*

I fell to my knees and begged.

The sharpest tap of his boot, catching me upon the throat, making me choke. *No.* He kicked me harder, again.

I yielded and said no more.

Scars on Sound

By this time, I was well tutored not only in pleasure and pain, but in its philosophy, its art. He had instructed me until I knew the things I longed for at his hands were perverse, shameful, unclean, had forced into my mind the knowledge that I was filthy, base, that I had no hope of redemption. This self-reproach amused him, as it amused him to have me kneel before him and confess, to spill out the debaucheries I performed at his commands, beseeching him to forgive me enough to come and use my body again. My whore's tongue licked willingly around these orisons of filth. I shed tears and begged him to come closer, to force my mouth against his crotch. Oh, I could speak so eloquently of asceticism, of denial of the flesh, of my lost honour, while my body ached to his absence. Most nights, eventually, he would relent. I would be desperate, willing to do anything, to do things I would repeat, voice shaking with lust, at the next night's confession.

But perhaps you would rather I were victim, some virgin wronged. I see you, the sheets pulled up to your chin, your lips half opened in some excuse, some platitude. Do not let me deceive you in this. I was not innocent in the matter. Whatever he wished to give me, I received with thanks. I do not deserve your pity. If I speak the truth, I still find pleasure in the shame.

Yes. Shame. Those hard memories: as when I realised my father had put a watch upon my bedchamber, that my Lord had been seen. I had been far too much the fool to realise that any maid, any footman would have recognised him. They had watched him leave by my window, marked the rings upon his hands, the crest upon his horse. It transpired the watcher had also heard my confession, my rendition of my beloved sins, and she would no longer look me in the eye. My father was angry, of course, but this rage once so monumental, so feared, fell to nothing as I thought of the ice that burnt in my Lord's eyes, the cuts that burnt across my body.

Still, my father stormed, all bluster, *I shall kill the fiend. I shall call him out and pierce his bestial heart.*

I pleaded that he did not.

He has dishonoured my daughter and my name. Sullied you, child, sullied you wilfully, cruelly, yet you protect him? What hold does this man have on you?

I knew my Lord would expect me to defend him, to swear that it was I who had led him astray, that it was my perverse lust that called our midnight meetings. I ached to do so, but even my father would not have believed my Lord a woman's slave.

In your condition no other man will have you, there were tears so close to anger's edge, *if you so fear him that you will not leave him, prevail upon his black heart to take you in marriage. If you cannot, I shall destroy him.*

I turned my night-bleached eyes away, too afraid to argue any longer. Always, and always, I have been too afraid.

He laughed. *This again?* I had come to his own house and surprised him into a pleasant mood. *I may have to beat it out of you.*

I asked again.

He advanced upon me, the whip in his hand in deadly earnest.

I wished to cease, to lie down, obedient and silent. My voice came in a rush of fear, "You must."

Must? His hand was in my hair and he twisted it to a rope that tugged my eyes to weeping agony. The menace of his voice sent a shudder through me, *Must take a wife with your base skills?*

"I am with child, sir." I must have shouted it, or screamed.

Liar.

His anger was cold, piercing cold, like the wind that swept down from the moors of my childhood, like the snow that does not melt upon your corpse. In what followed, he did not lose that coldness. What he lost was the distance, the elegance in his cruelty. His face became almost ugly.

Why, you deceitful bitch.

He yanked my hair up, pulling the skin too tight for my

eyes to close in pain. I must have pleaded, although I do not remember it. For a moment, he stared, his look searing my face with the chill that will be your death on a lonely hillside. My hair felt that it might come loose.

"Sir. I am not lying." Was it a whimper? A plea for belief?

The first blow caught me quicker and harder than I could breathe.

At the next blow, hurt licked through me with none of its usual pleasure. My body, my mind curled inwards at this blunt, brutal torture. The thorns of his voice tore my skin, *If that's true take it to the man who put it in you.*

A pause.

Or shall I save him the trouble?

He had never beaten me as hard as he did then, never kicked and whipped, never spat or sworn in that way. Curled upon the ground, I wondered why I loved him. Yet still as I watched him, intent upon destroying the poor wretch at his feet, I wanted him. He could have been an angel, vehement in retribution.

My hands raised in prayer, "Please."

He laughed and his boot caught my cheekbone. My vision blurred to blood.

"Kill me."

What?

I choked on the blood that blocked my throat, that crept up my nose, that flooded my lungs. "If you wish to kill me, kill me," I must have been sobbing, I cannot remember, "but my child is yours."

No, his face paled in what, in another man, might have been fear, *that cannot be.*

"I will lie, if that is what you want."

He shook his head. His pallor did not change. When he touched me next, he was almost tender.

I began to cry. The pain was duller than it had been although it still stripped my flesh to the bones. "My father will call you out."

Don't threaten.

"He said if you have ruined me, he shall ruin you." The distance between us ached against my torn skin.

My Lord nodded. He thought as I lay and bled, then his eyes flickered to me with contempt and lust.

My bare back burnt against the cold of the marble floor. Blood seeped from me. His rings were cold, metallic, hard against my lips, his voice hoarse as rawhide as he whispered that perhaps I was honest, perhaps I was true, but if I betrayed him, if I deceived him, if I disobeyed him ever, he would kill me. My answer was silenced by sharp teeth around my throat, but I would have told him his judgement was welcome, just.

These dark nights are the worst, by far. You see the way the moon comes uneven through the clouds? How the bed swallows the light? Yes, these dark nights are the worst, for I expect him to be here and cannot see where he might be.

Alys Earl

This house is as dark as his heart and all is cold, cold as a hanged man's tomb, rough as the rope, rough as poorly woven sheets...

It troubles me that I have found you here, in this room.

But see how hard the stone seems in this light?

He will not come. These are chambers he has abandoned, used and discarded, like my body. My body on our wedding night.

Yes, our wedding was a sorrowful affair. A wonder I had not lost the child, with the beating and the corset that hid my condition. My Lord was unconcerned, my father broken-hearted. Only the priest seemed fervent as he blessed us both, as he extolled the virtues of marriage. Even I felt scorn, the lead paint thick and lying over the bruises on my face, as he spoke of the sanctity, the care. My love's lip was curled in perfect derision. My father whispered to me, before he gave me away, *You are dead to me.*

Those were the last words I heard him say.

Scars on Sound

Afterwards, I did not cry. When he took me, in the hall, where the servants could watch, took me with all his sensual brutality, with all the usual blood and pain, I enjoyed what was offered and did not ask for more. He tore my wedding dress to shreds with his knife, left me kneeling in only my stockings before he gestured to a maid to take me away. So my position changed. My room became a cramped chamber in the attics where the servants slept, the bed rough, wretched, small. There was a bar from which my few gowns hung, and a bell with which he summoned me. The servants held me in contempt, me, called me the bachelor's wife, and my Lord was absent most of the day. The pornography he owned was scant consolation; in glancing through its pictures and its text I thought only of him.

Sometimes, at night, he would have me recite what I had learnt and would whip me, saying no decent wife would read such things. Sometimes, then, he would forgive me. And some nights he humiliated me, calling me down to where he lay with one of his whores, calling upon me to serve her, bring her food, drink, whatever she might desire. Blindly, willingly

I obeyed. His boredom was apparent and it was desperation that made me chase the few scraps of interest he cared to show. This, he knew.

Soon, though, my time came. He had watched my body grow, become grotesque, and soon his whores, his servants, were sent away. They questioned the order no more than I would have done. He allowed me, then, to approach the marriage bed, to perform small duties to ease his lust. The peace of that time seduced me, filled me with the prayer that this was how it would remain after his son was born.

Son? True, there was no way I could know, but I was certain that the thing that stretched and kicked within me was a boy, a boy who would grow as powerful and devastating as his father. Perhaps, I hoped, when I had given him that proof, he would accept me again and...

I apologise. Please, I am quite well. But I would ask why you were sleeping here? Whose words directed you to this room? For it was there, where you stand beside the bed, that I bore his son for him.

And is it not strange how, in the dark, this chamber seems almost a sepulchre, a place to store the bones of the dead? Surely, there are pleasanter lodgings to which you could be brought?

For when the pangs came, I paced, crouched, screamed. My first delivery, bewildering and unknown. Yet I knew better than to beg the kindness of a midwife. Only his cold eyes watched as I struggled and gasped and flinched. My cries arched up and threw themselves against the ceilings, battering themselves to echoed silence against cold veins of marble. My back felt it would break while he lay upon the bed, propped on his arms. It was the voyeur in him, to observe me as I became one pulsing muscle of pain, one tunnelling scream beyond agony and despair.

I cannot say how long, how long I cried, how long my body thrust new life through itself, but it ended, as all things must end.

The child flopped out, small and wrinkled as a corpse that has drowned, the child of sin and lust, stained with blood and lying exhausted in my shaking arms. I turned to him, holding out his son. He swung himself round, his beauty shining, and I did not care. The cord still snaked, heavy and sore between my thighs. My heart beat to the tiny thing in my arms. My husband smiled at me, smiled at the boy, smiled the cold, winter's smile that pierced my heart like a bolt of hate, and threw me his dagger in its sheath. I used it to cut the cord and clutched my baby to me again. The after-birth spilled out onto the floor. My husband lent towards me and laid his hand upon the baby's head. He licked his lips and whispered, *Kill the brat*.

His voice was like a lick of pain, a kiss of agony, the taste of a sin for which I no longer cared.

"No," I dropped the knife to the ground, "This is your son."

And you are my wife, he lifted the blade again, handing it to me by the hilt. His smile had edged into a sharp-toothed grimace of threat, *as such, it is I you should obey.*

It was fear, not adoration, which drove me. I turned and

Scars on Sound

I laid my baby beside the afterbirth, plunging the blade down, once, then again, again. The dagger slipped from my hand, all smeared with blood. I was crying, but I did not scream. The scream remained inside me. It is there still.

One white finger caressed my cheek. I longed to flinch away but he lifted up my face until I stared into his. The evil there passed through me. It killed.

He took me to the bed and I went, hating each exhausted movement, hating all that lay about me, hating his blood-slicked hands between my legs, in my hair. I hated his kisses, their invasion of this sacrilege.

The child's cry betrayed me.

Of course it did. I knew little of these things. Laid on the cold floor, away from comfort and breast, it was only natural the boy should start to wail. My hair became the rope he used to haul my head back as though in readiness for the killing blade. But he did not let me die as a noblewoman at the swordsman's blow. No, I was not to die like that.

You have betrayed me, the first blow, *for him?* Again the taste of blood, the smell sickening me, a boot kicking my torn, bleeding crotch. I stumbled back, away, desperate, towards my child's cries. Calm, impassive, monstrous, he stepped between us. *He dies anyway,* he said, and he reached down and lifted our child, the screaming thing that flailed so, the little thing I wanted to press to my breast and protect and he laughed as he dashed it to the floor, laughed until our son was no more than a pile of blood and bones. Then he turned to me, that smile still in his eyes, his voice like midwinter's ice. I wanted to scream, to scream until the sound was a wall between me us, but his voice could cut even that.

Without your treachery, his death would have been swift.

And with those words it was gone, gone as if it had never been. The spell resumed, left my body hollow, bewildered, sore. I felt only shame. Yes, shame and, to my eternal shame, my lust for him returned even as that blood pooled around his feet, pooled over the cold marble of the floor. I fell to my knees, crawled through that tangle of ruined flesh towards him, but as I came near the flash of his whip, the toe of his boot repelled me. I lifted bloody hands towards him, "My Lord, my love-"

He sneered into my beseeching face. *Leave.*

"My Lord —"

Go. The word was sharper than a kick in its reprimand. I flinched, seeing the blood glinting crimson upon the soft, fine leather of his boots. I tried to lick it away, as I had when the blood had been mine. He kicked my mouth. *You attempted to deceive me,* his voice soft, caressing, even as the blows became harder, *the blame is yours.*

"Then kill me."

He walked away. I felt his disdain congeal upon my lips, turning my pleas, my promises into thorns, thorns stinging my tongue. Like a dog, I scrabbled across the bloodstained marble floor.

He did not even turn to me. I reached out a hand, but he kicked it away. *I have no further need of you.*

Weak and aching, my body in shock, my back burning from his blows, I cried. I needed that rude, earthly pain to leave me, needed to be in his presence, to cling to him. I needed his love wrapped around me, turning this shame, this horror into beautiful sin, but he had withdrawn whatever scant regard I had once possessed. After some time I stood and walked to the room that had been mine. There, the sheets were coarse against my skin, chafing the memory of who I had been before he had stolen me with a kiss, a waltz, chafing as I wrapped that makeshift rope about my neck and took the lurching drop I hoped would bring me peace.

He told them that I died in childbirth, that our child miscarried, dragging me with it to the grave. But he is the one that killed me, killed me with a cold smile and a colder heart, killed me by leaving me there in this bloody chamber. All I keep now from my youth is the silence he once smiled upon, for I rarely speak as I wander his shadows, as I last this eternity that should be sleep. My nightmare, that is what he is. He has come and gone and returned again, and I have watched it all. I have seen the women he has brought here and destroyed. Rarely, I will speak to them. As long as he lasts, as long as this place lasts, I will be here.

You could say I walk in penitence or in hope of revenge; that I mourn, that this is sorrow, but that would not be true. I am condemned to this, damned. Even then, it is not as you think. Not for foolishness, for suicide, for any sin. No.

I am damned because I love him still.

Grimm's Law

Another ghost story? Well.

His name was not Adler, but that was what they called him.

But no. That makes no sense without the right inflection, without that accent half a century dead. Imagine a language of cropped words, one that takes in consonants like an old coat and uses the spare to patch out rural vowels. Or so I might guess from its descendent, the thing touches my throat when I speak in anger, speed or pain.

They called him Adler. He lived up the hill.

Which hill? Of course. Our language presumes there are so many hills, but this story is a dialect that knows only one, one draping up the valley from the Medway's pulse, past the Redstart and the old mental hospital. It is not steep, not so very steep, yet houses straggle from it like weary travellers. One road crawls up it, changing its name with rural economy,

Alys Earl

South Street becoming North. There, at just the point where that happens, is the war memorial. Look down. Below you, Kettle Bridge. On your left, a village bleeding into a town. On your right, the kind of fields that make me heartsick if I think of them too long. And the memorial, shaped like a cross. No doubt it was on her mind, my Great-Grandmother's, the day that I was born, the day she told my Father she was glad I was a girl, that my sister and I both were girls.

Further up the hill, the village carries on. I know it through my Father's stories, a private map that lends each stopping point a shadow. So it is high up, near woods that echo with campfires and woodbine stems smoked in lieu of real cigarettes, that we find old Adler's house.

Or we would have done, then.

An old man, old family. Mr Adler it should have been, the money should have bought that, but Old Adler was what they called him, perhaps even to his face. Names, titles get no more reverence than phonemes. My Grandmother has a cousin buried out in Italy and I could not tell you what is written on his grave.

Scars on Sound

"We called him Boy. Everyone just called him Boy."

And what of Old Adler? Well, he'd once had a wife.

Maybe it was childbirth did for her. Or influenza, or some other thing, the kind of illness that doesn't kill you any more. I cannot name her, either, must give her up to that faceless fate of women dead. We tell stories about the dead for the same reason we build monuments to them: appeasement. We run their tragedies like beads between our fingers until their features are worn quite away, as though our mumble of generic words keeps them safe within their graves. The dead are dangerous when unmourned.

Yet why do we fear their hauntings when none of us believe in ghosts?

No. Wait. No. This is important.

We are not credulous in these tales, not given to superstition. These stories are told, always, with a caveat, their protagonist defined by disbelief. "Your Great-Grandmother, who was not a fanciful woman, was said to have The Sight."

Still, God knows the supernatural had material enough. Each generation in my family has a missing child: a stillbirth, a cot-death, or who knew what – another of those things that doesn't kill you any more. Hard years, and sentiment is a commodity that does not come cheap. Up the hill, the farm labourers' cottages make squat rows: walls one brick thick, narrow windows that never catch the light. Parlour, kitchen, privy out the back. No space for mawkishness in rooms like that, no money for it, either. When my Great-Grandmother found the sovereign that slotted into another ghost story, it was treated like any other money. A gunshot from a lorry's cab will burst a pheasant's head.

The things we kill, we eat.

And yet, yet, yet, rabbit was the one meat my Grandmother would never touch, even in the hard years, even in the War. Wisps and shreds of tender-heartedness clutched tight against the century's blood.

Old Adler died alone.

So many ways that one could be alone, and he all of

them. No wife, no family, no will. His house was knocked down and over it they laid dreams of semi-detached rusticity. The village exhaled, slumped into fields, allotments and heritage sites. I live in a house like that, now, half a country from the hill and half a century away. From my window, writing this, I can just see fields that look so little like the fields of my home.

Anyway. They tore down old Adler's place in the years when my Grandfather had been to Suez and come back again with the pride of his Sergeant, the beginnings of skin cancer, and the memories of his dead mates. The village was not, not quite, the kind of place you did not know your neighbours' names.

You would have known my Grandfather, anyway. A shade over six foot with a warrior's name. A Special Constable. He'd lied about his age to sign up in the Second Lot and took his National Service afterwards without complaint. He would only speak of it as a joke, a boast. Men like him do not have words for PTSD. Too strong for that, a marksman and a hero.

The kind of man who helped out when the river was in flood, who fixed his own roof right into his seventies.

Even we didn't know until the heart-attacks. Before that, he was too busy with police work, with being the parish council's Chair. No time to pause when times are hard. No ghosts, no sentiment, no PTSD.

Even so.

One Wednesday night with the council session done, one of the girls came over to him and asked who'd had her house before she did.

She weren't a local girl, not *local* local, but when we get into the grit of things, neither was he. His mother's maiden name was Lee, his grandfather was Romany. The family had held land out on Grain, up near the estuary. Still, he'd married a local girl and he pitched in. You could count on him. So it was that this girl, this interloper, this resident of fifties brick, asked him who it was who'd had her house before she did.

"Well, it's new built," my Grandfather said. But as he thought on it, the old shape of things poked up its bones, "Though it might be it's over Old Adler's place."

"Right," she says, and works her nails into her hands, the varnish on them the faintest, most tasteful of pinks. She's in her housecoat and her perm is set, and she'll not say the word "haunted", no. Not even she. "Thing is, we hear it at night. Someone walking about there. Downstairs. Talking, like. I come down but there's no-one there. But you can hear him. Crying, almost."

So my Grandfather got out the plans and lined them up, and that was how he knew.

The thing is, Old Adler died intestate. And while it's the government's business if they're getting the lot, they had more important things to worry them right then, so, it was a good long time before they told a local boy he was charged as executor. It was his job to tie up all Adler's business, his job to clear the house.

It was good stuff, too. Besides, the government's got no

business troubling quiet folk. So he took his barrow up the hill and loaded it with everything that weren't nailed down.

And it weren't like he weren't generous with it. They all got bits and pieces, and by "they", I mean "we". Heirlooms guarantee my complicity. Besides, it weren't all that much. A nice bit of china and, wrapped up inside it, this story. Because, you see, as he made his pillage of the place he found a door he couldn't open. Found a room all shuttered and locked.

The only thing for it was to force the door. It took more than one man to do it.

He'd been a quiet man, Old Adler. The kind of man you mean when you talk of someone keeping to himself. Long hours spent alone, not gardening, nor shooting like men ought. Too old for both wars, and in a locked room in his house?

A shrine.

No, it's not much of a story. Perhaps you wanted

something that would look better on a front page, some Bluebeard's Chamber, some Tell-Tale Heart. Something Gothic and proper and scary, rather than clothes, trinkets and photographs. Because there were so many pictures, pictures of his wife.

Well, I'm sorry if I've denied you that squirm, that distant terror, but...

Look: between the wars there was no money, no work, no meat. Some men feigned madness because in the nuthouse you got three meals a day. Then, after the Second Lot, the country, the continent, the world was still an open wound. Chatham had it bad, and London was a bombed wreck. Africa, India, the Middle East were being hacked about and sent along a course all primed for massacre. My Great-Uncle was there the day they liberated Belsen.

And Adler? In Adler's house there was a *shrine*.

When he died, they ripped the place apart.

You'd think that would silence him, wouldn't you? That

this would rip it out, that last decadence, that final shred of the Victorian world?

But when they got the plans, you see, when the got the plans to that girl's front room, with its fitted carpet and the plastic runners to keep things clean, that little temple to a future where tractors crept shrinking fields and machines pulled down the hop binds, it matched. Wall for wall, pace for pace, it matched with Adler's shrine.

So does it matter? Does it matter my Grandfather's accent got swallowed up by its urban twin? Does it matter they took even that from my Father the day they sent him to Barton Road? Does it make it a fair swap for some Latin, some poetry, a love of Beckett's plays? Does it matter that laws changed and my Grandfather took all his guns, yes, all of them, yes, even the little pearl-handled pistol he looted in Suez, and gave them to the police?

And now? Well, were I there, I could cross Kettle Bridge and walk up South Street, past the railway line. I could cross the road and hear whispers from the war memorial. I could

Scars on Sound

follow North Street all the way to the house where my Father was born. And my memory would twist things, would put stories too high, too low, on the wrong side of the road. I might see ghosts, for all I don't believe in them, but they would be ghosts misplaced and misconstrued. For all that, I could walk on, right up to The Redstart and the quarry thick with trees. When I got there, I could turn and look down at the valley, at the hop fields as we lose them, the fields of wheat and sheep. I could look upriver to Teston, where my Mother's Grandfather kept the lock, and when I had done all that, I could tell you stories; the greatest part of my inheritance.

But the names on the memorial are unknown to me, just as I do not know the colour of Boy's eyes. I couldn't point you to the house where Adler wept out an afterlife and I do not know if he is weeping still. On both sides of the road the houses are red brick and smart, and there are more of them where I think orchards still stand. Double-glazed and heated centrally. From them, commuters flow, up and down the hill, as steady as the Medway in my veins.

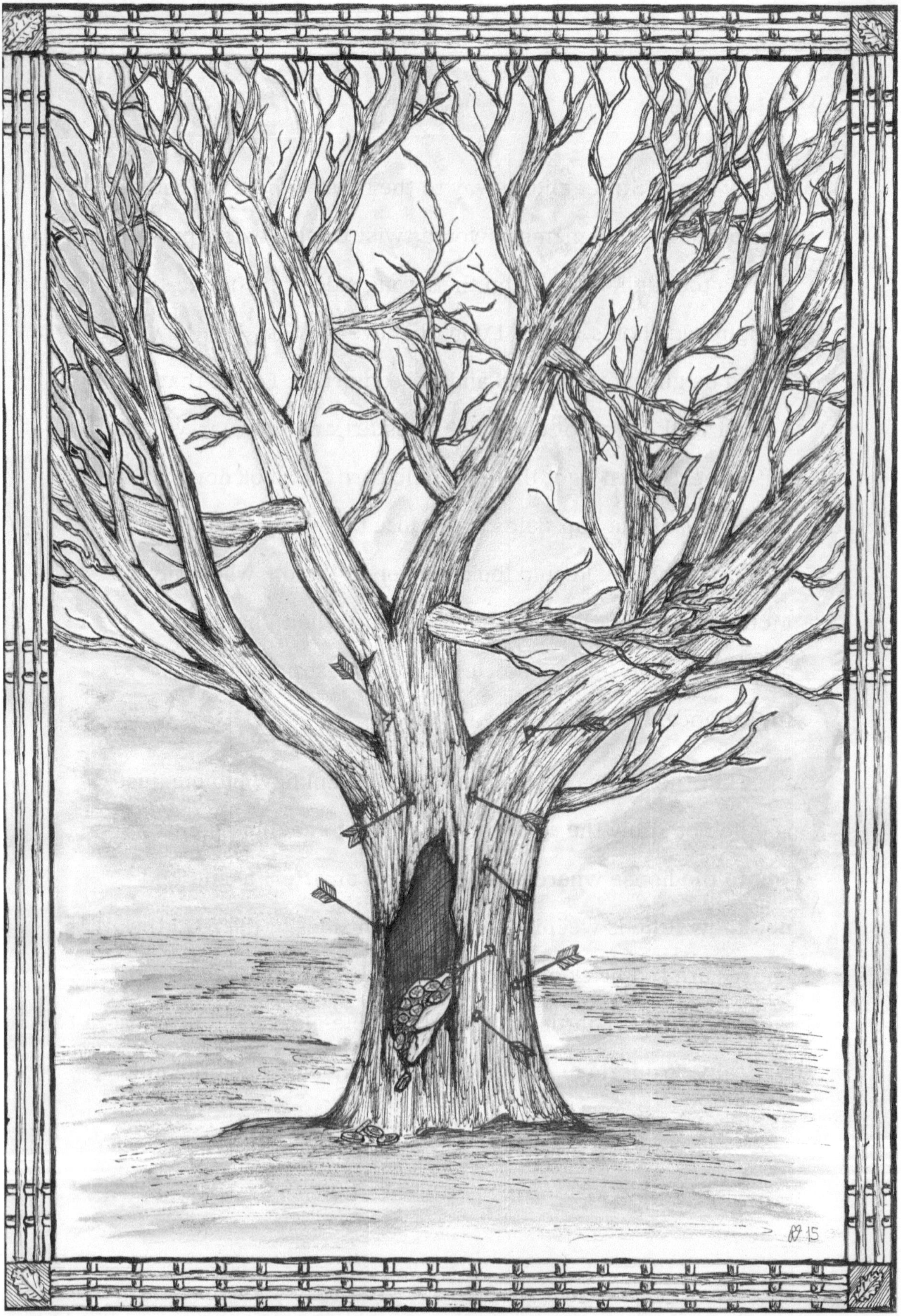

The Song of Bill o'Dale

My true love has left my hall

Following the hunting call

Of those that flee the city's walls

Among the leaves so green, O.

All her life there had been whisper and cant until he became part hero, part saint. Bill o'Dale gone to the greenwood with his wife, sending back the currents of his gests until the town rang with them, until it seemed that bramble and dog rose curled along the shit-strewn streets.

There had been, too, the slow stream of vagrants as the patchwork of arable vanished beneath pasture's smooth green and, each evening at the hearth, rumour splashing down upon her as her father and his friends thought that she did not attend them.

"I tell you, it's Chat all over again," that name, whispered in private with all the fervency of prayer, for all that the law would call him traitor, criminal. Her father, most of all, would invoke him, remembering his uncle's tales of the commotion time, the Constitution Oak. "They took Norwich —"

"And Ferrour's men took the Tower. They still took Tyler's head."

Her father's house was his pride, a shabby token of prosperity leaning over the stalls and tenements of the market. So it puzzled her to see his sidelong glance along its walls, as though the timbers and daub might betray him. "Chat's men weren't wild Tylerians. They were driven to the fray, they did not —"

"Too much of what we hear of Tyler is a lie."

And in childhood she had been content to let it lie at that, to clutch the second, secret rosary her parents shared: Tyler, Lister, Ball, good Robbie Chat. For years it was no more than the broad, smooth shape of heroism. She did not wonder at it, just as she did not wonder at the families come begging a coin, or how, despite the laws forbidding vagrancy, men would still say, "I know these people. Good men, thrown from the land."

Scars on Sound

Once, within her hearing, an old man nodded, "Those are Dale's men."

"They don't wear green."

A shrug. "They'll go to the woods, child. What else do they have?"

For who should seek to find him here
where women labour year on year
to bake and brew and speak small beer
Among the leaves so green, O.

Then the day the ballad crowders stood, words throttled in their throats, when from Stratford they had the news that Bill o'Dale was dead. She had leaned from the windows to hear it, her work falling to her feet as she flung back the shutters to catch rumour's rush and roar: "His side pierced in a forest glen…"

"…the King's men…?"

"No, no, murdered in his bed, loosing an arrow to mark where his body would lie…"

The day had no rest for her. She twitched and twisted, straining for news. At their looms and counters, her father's 'prentices and labourers whispered, intrigued, but they would stop their gossip at her approach. Only Will would take her hand, would say, "Bill o'Dale is captured."

She glanced about, made furtive by the news, the touch, "Dead?"

"No, London. They'll do this by the law."

And as though this confidence had marked her one of them, another said, "They'll take him through the Traitor's Gate before they're done."

The air was hot with breath spent in quiet talk. Outside the town walls, the wheat hung pale and heavy, ready for the scythe. She recalled her grandmother's tales of Jack Lister, seized as he hid among the blowing corn.

Scars on Sound

She's let her seam fall to the floor,

Slipped past the eyes that guard the door,

Why should his liberty than hers be more

Among the leaves so green, O?

Winter. A dead time. Smoke in the houses, mud freezing in the streets. Her father's workshop clacked with looms, with fingers chafed and frost-bitten. No-one spoke of Bill o'Dale, hanging in his gibbet at the Tower. They logged the cost of fleece, the price of thread. In church, men wore caps of white and filled the alms boxes with money from that same trade. On the land, strip farms were put to profitable pasture. Old men spat in the streets: "Devil take this wool."

But with the first breath of spring, the songs returned, calling to the greenwood and the wild. Her father sighed, "Camping time, commotion time." And as though his words had painted it, it came rushing in from the fields:

The site is bound that should be free,

the right is holden from the commonality...

As the trees unfurled the tales poured in, just as Chat's men had poured into the City from the heath, tales of how May Day wooing was scattered by the crowds who took their way to the fields, how the mattocks were raised up and hedges were torn down. In the streets that she might not walk alone, there were cries of "Dale's men," of, "All in Shaxbeard's name." His songs were shouted, the force of the words burning through the half-evading guise of love.

And she found she had a lover of her own.

With her parents' tacit nods, they stole half private moments and found — in their absence — the match had been settled upon, agreed. Yet Will was, at heart, a yeoman's son. So when he took her hand, cocooned by trade and town, by the future his parents had bought for him, she felt the struggle in him. Saw how he felt the weight of his prosperity as his friends, his neighbours lost their lease upon the land. He would even weep, as though to her alone he could bear to make himself emasculate.

"Greed," he would say, "There's nothing to this but

worldly greed. Pious Tresham will be dragged to hell by all that fleece." And he had pulled his hand from hers, held it out flat before her, marked by its years of 'prentice work. "Look at this honest trade of mine. The great woolpack, the King's gold bag, the country's wealth. Won't I do well from it, sweeting? Yet at night, I smell the wool fat on my hands like sin."

The song spun through the summer. It made the crowds, drew out the cries, and levelled the enclosure. It birthed rumour and dream, and it played so loud it drowned out all other sounds, even the prose from London, its stark and unforgiving text. It did not matter that the King struggled with his cousins, that the Tudors scrapped after the throne. The young King sent his proclamation and it demanded that this same text be nailed to the post of the gallows it ordered erected beside the market cross. Those that could read the Blackletter of it spoke it out to those who could not, and its words did not shift a syllable however many mouths spoke it. Undeniable, it gave its authority to the long finger of punishment casting its shadow on the bustle of the stalls.

Undeniable, it gave a boundary to what had been transient, ill-defined. It made a boundary, an enclosure of meaning against which the commons could raise its call.

From her father's doorway, she watched them tear the gallows down, watched the crowd sing as it ripped the King's command to tatters. Will burst from the throng as it surged past, his face mud-streaked, lip bleeding from the crush, and he raised his head and roared, "Common Law! We ask but Common Law!"

As he passed, he snatched her by the hand and dragged her from the safety of the house. Around them, song spilled and wound:

Our commons that at Lammas should be cast,
They are closed in and hedged full fast.

Jostled and shoved, she heard her father's tales, of how the rich trembled when we came roaring down from Mousehold, how it had been a City of itself, raised above the City on Saint James' Mount. "It's what the noblesse don't understand," he had said to Will, one night, while she fixed her eyes upon her work, "when the commotion men sat beneath that oak, the City had no choice but to fall. The will of the commonality." That last said as though it might be sufficient in itself, and she plied her needle over cloth, and did not understand.

But now, a loud echo to the whisper in her head, Will cried, "You see? They can do nothing! Tresham and Montague and the magistrate's men? For all their enclosure and their deer runs and their flock, we can bear down on them like a wave."

Beside him, she had believed it.

The tallest oak within this glade
Pluck't by its roots and down is laid
To give my true love's bow'r its shade
Among the leaves so green, O.

With the mayflower still frothing on the trees and sunlight struggling its early brightness she ran to the enclaves muttering on corners and in alleyways. The oak leaves trembled sour green and the old wives gathered them to brew into wine. The streets were ploughed to mud, her clogs teetered through the dung and stink, her skirt was stained and soiled. Conversations were things of snatches, gasps. "What power have they without Tyburn's tree?"

"...seek not to destroy, but build, make us Yeoman all, upon the common land."

"...clear out the weeds, level the enclosure. It's what any good farmer would tell you."

"How can it be treason? All we ask is a new commons..."

By the time they met on Newton's plain, they were no longer Tylerians or Commotion Men but Diggers, Levellers. They tore the hedges, filled the ditches and stood, at last, in long rows as the command to disperse was read once, then once again. She clutched Will's hand and with the other gripped her staff. The militia faced them, faces blank, their culpability concealed by their liveries, their masters' commands. They carried real weapons, expensive, new.

Whispers hissed up and down the line.

"...men like us, common men..."

"... under his protection, they won't feel any need to stay their hands."

"Our quarrel's not with them."

"...defy them and Tresham's maintenance, too."

Spit was bitter in her mouth. The muscles in her neck ached from the clenching of her jaw.

Beside her in the crowd, an old man said, "Don't give them reason to charge."

The voice of the herald was reedy with distance, half lost in the protesting calls, the shifting of feet, but they knew its sense. To abandon this, to accept defeat and to return to their homes.

"Not on your life," Will whispered, his knuckles pale as he locked his hand around her own.

For no reason that she understood, she answered him with song, quiet and high, "My true love has fled my hall…"

Those around her caught the catch, and threw it up, a tattered chorus, a ragged protest pouring from one man's mind, burying itself like seeds into the thoughts of thousands. In that moment, it was as through the quickening had come, as though frail green shoots were stirring up towards the sun.

Then the militia charged.

Violent instinct stole her hand from Will's. The lines surged, crushed together, and she heard as scythe and club and pole found their mark in flesh. She fought. Knuckles skinned and bruised. Ribs cracked with kicks and shoves. The wind was pounded from her, once, twice, too many times to count. Veil torn from her head, hair yanked and wild, she could not see to strike. Faces blurred. Stones and sticks clattered through the crush as the greensward under them was trampled to mud.

No glimpse of Will.

She stood her ground, faced forward, fought. She had not known she could. Breath gasped sore in her chest. She saw a skull cracked, a woman fall to ground. Coldly, clearly desperate, she swore and she blasphemed and stood her ground.

Every one of them stood their ground.

Time returned in gasps between the bruising and the blood and the crush grew less, the fighting giving way to whispers up and down the lines, "We held."

"Yes, we held."

"The militia are in retreat."

Her fingers found her blackened eye, found places where skin had spread and split upon her brow. She spat blood to the earth. Again, the whisper rustling through the air, "Stand firm."

Teeth aching, stomach sick with it. Her knuckles leaked thin trails of water and blood. Bones shone through her skin. She clenched her staff and tasted fury, tasted light.

Alys Earl

The next charge broke the line.

And far from the law's stern report,
We find freedom to disport,
In morning light and merry thought,
Among the leaves so green, O.

Diggers shoved and struggled and were cut down. The song that they had shared was crushed by running feet. Limbs loose, head a swelling point of pain, she fled. A young man fell across her path. She hauled him to his feet and they staggered on to the shelter of a stand of trees. Behind them, chaos surged, the rout becoming screams that stabbed the summer air. She tripped on a root, crashed hard onto the earth. She could not move, could not force her arms to raise her. Through the long hours to dusk she lay, sharp chips of enamel cutting her gums from where her teeth had cracked.

At last, in darkness, she began to journey to her father's house. Two days in the company of hunger, pain and thirst. Blood-grimed and torn, she stumbled in and wept until sleep claimed her. The next day, she ran her rosary through her fingers and found that she could not recall a single prayer. She washed and dressed her bruises, waited for news.

The dead numbered forty at least.

They said, too, that the leaders had been taken, but she recalled no leaders when they had stood on Newton's plain. Still, their names would take their place in the litany of the Commons, with Cade and Chat and Bill o'Dale. The rest, the rumours claimed, would receive pardon.

"Of course," she spat, hard and rough round broken teeth, "they could never hang us all."

There was no news of Will.

The trials began on Midsummer's Day. The verdict and sentence surprised no-one. Drawn, quartered, hanged, the broken bodies displayed about the town, a warning written out in text one need not be a scholar to read. There was talk of a submission to be signed, a general pardon's sole condition.

"Why," she would have asked, had Levellers still seethed on street corners, "are we willing to settle for this?" But ravens picked at bloody flesh, and 'prentices met and plotted no more.

She was surprised that she was unafraid. She had expected to feel it, as she had felt it in the battle, in the retreat. Instead, it seemed as though someone had struck an axe into her heart, as though hope, fervour and trepidation had been destroyed by uncaring blows. In the woods, the oaks were dusty, dark. Small acorns swelled in summer rains. The streets of Leicester were empty, foul.

No news of Will.

When the day came to sign the submission, she walked away. Strange how easy it was to leave security, respectability. Yes, a voice in her cried out, shrieked of vagrancy, treason, rape, but it fell silent because in her the silence was absolute. No song carried her as she rejected the walls that had so long preserved her comfort, her reputation. She turned south, to London, to the sea. There was half a thought that she would take her quarrel to the King, that she would walk to the Tower Johanna Ferrour had stormed, the place where Shaxbeard and Chat had been hanged.

There was half a thought that she would cast herself into the Thames.

Behind her, she left silence; silence in Newton, Mousehold, Stratford, Kent.

Every village she passed, each town, was further proof. Undisputed hedges ringed the fields of sheep and wanderers trailed in hungry groups. More than once, she passed the press gangs, their victims bundled, unconscious, drunk. She learned to conceal herself from them as she would hide from the Sheriff's men.

And soon, her destination came to her. She would go to the woods. What else did she have?

Her feet blistered, her back stiffened from a bed of earth. She accepted hunger, hardship, cold. And as she did, she caught the strollers' songs, the blacksmith singing at his forge, the women driving geese to market and every one of them called out in testimony which no ear could deny, no gallows ever strangle, *"Among the leaves so green, O..."*

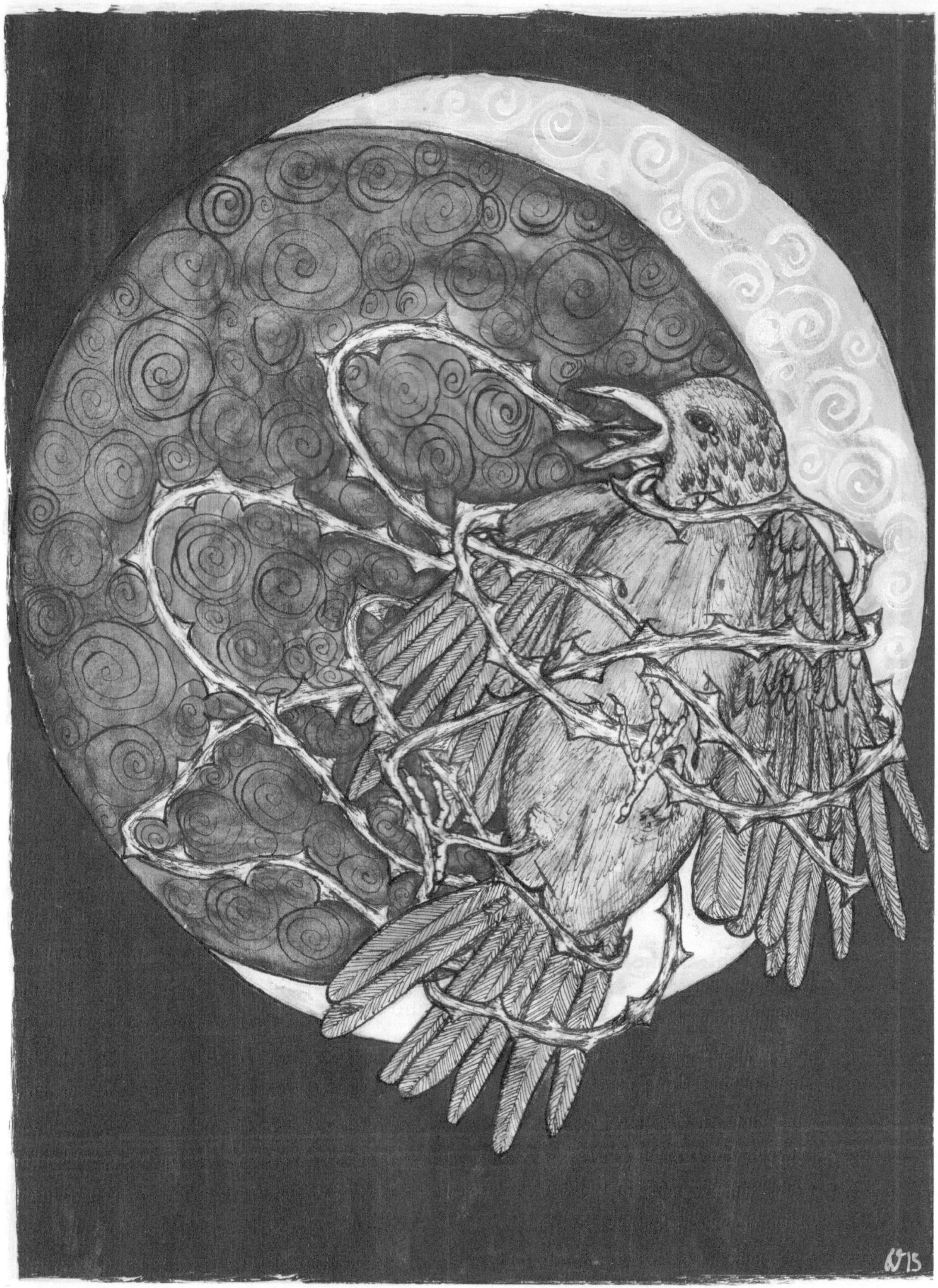

The Maternal Line

The woman walked the track from the village to where the hanged man swung.

It was calmer there, but she could hear a yelping from the heights, as though of dogs. The body dripped cold urine from the bladder's last release. She was not an old woman, but the climb left her breathless. Resting in the gallows shade she coughed and thought of her daughter, grown and with a daughter of her own, safe from this spreading pool of blood.

She climbed the tree, took the knife from her pocket and used it to saw the rope. She did not wish for him to fall as a shot hawk but she had no ally who would take his burden, no helpmeet. The noose cut deep into his neck. Above his right eye, a gash left by some blunt instrument. There was a stab wound spreading bloody on the left side of his chest.

She had thought she was without emotion, but as he dropped, as she scrambled down beside him and cradled his fractured skull, she was surprised by tears, by the way they made salt circles in the blood that clotted his hair, and over the freckles thick upon his cheeks.

When she had wept herself raw, she searched his pockets for the photograph that should be there but all she found was a keepsake of herself, a faded image, a lock of hair.

The earth was sharp with bracken, the cold like cruel hands at weary joints. There was a smell of wood-smoke, the sound of wind among trees. When she heard the footsteps on the path, she turned and looked up into her father's eyes.

"We'll give him a Christian burial," Jack Gower said, as though it had not been almost three decades since they had spoken, "though it's more than he deserves."

Behind him were the old boys from the village. They took the body from her, lifted him on their shoulders and bore him down to the red stone church, leaving her alone with a photo of herself she was afraid to crumple. There was a life waiting for her and she could return to it, but there was so much more of herself bound up in this place, in the sea's whisper and the picture of her that he had carried to his death. Caught, uncertain, she gave a sigh that took twenty-one years to reach the village, twenty-one years to brush the cheek of the vicar who sat in the New Rectory with a book of sermons before him. It lay upon his blameless cheek like the whisper of frost, and he recalled the girl who had come to the graveyard the summer before, the girl who had vanished into the night.

*

Her grandmother never forgave the Poet.

Even when the emphysema had gnawed her lungs and stopped her voice, when she was confined to a hospital bed, clad in the tatters of a beauty that had shattered itself on lost ideals and gin, her eyes had kept a steady hatred, defying the tears and hugs of those who loved her.

That was not how she remembered Nan Gower, no. Nan Gower, still young and hoarse-voiced, holding a glass of gin with a cigarette propped between the first and second fingers as though unable to hear her daughter's exaggerated coughs.

"I were a flower child," she'd say, "back in the sixties. Before I met your granddad." She had even kept her old LPs in a box that she never opened, gorgeous, painted covers to winding, psychedelic tunes that were never played. "Run away from home, and I weren't much older than you. My dad were a dreadful old fart."

And her mother's desperate, brittle respectability, "Mum, I don't think Gwyneth need hear…"

Strange to think that had once been her name.

"Ah, don't listen to your mum. London in sixty-eight. Think of it, Gwyn. There was nowhere else to be. I went to London to," the unwinding blue from Nan Gower's unfiltered cigarettes, the slow dividing of a cancer no-one thought to diagnose, "it doesn't matter. I must have had a reason. Your granddad put me up, and before too long —" the pointed glance at Gwyneth's mother, the family scandal sidling in, and then the cough, low and vicious in her chest, the sip of gin to quiet it. When she had her breath again, she said, "It was Poet's fault, all of that. Never trust an enigmatic man, Gwyn.

Scars on Sound

Never fall in love with one."

*

It was calmer here. The night was stark and new. She stood on the hill, her body marked out by night winds, cold hands upon cold arms. When she had been born, the skin of her hands and wrists had been as bright and pink as flesh newly scarred.

From the moor, she could see the sea, could feel the rock beneath her, as bony and loving as a thin man's embrace.

The landscape greeted her, familiar as the curve of her breasts, hips, stomach. She could touch it with the same fingers, an affirmation of her boundaries, her solidity.

Her family had never come here. Not once in all her past life had she walked these rock pools and bays, the shale and alabaster cliffs, this loping moor, but it forgave her, bare feet on grasses winter-dead, wind grasping her like supporting hands. Spring crouched beneath the topsoil, a promise immutable, uneasy as the bones tidied away beneath the holy rock. Around her, the world reformed itself, moving her memories, making links and drawing concordances as clear as the sudden vision with which she saw the patterns in the stars. In the wood, the winter leaves would be gone halfway to mould, the wind would scratch itself against the trees. The landscape touched her lips with history and she saw her path open before her.

As she came down from the heights, the moon tilted in the sky, bright as a polished bow.

*

He would fall on the hill.

Last night, hands torn and sore from graveyard raging, he had burned the great oak table, the last piece of furniture in his parents' house. Now, he lay on the floor by the ashes, his fingers wrapped in knots, the way he had once knotted a dead man's belt. He felt young, raw. He felt that if he closed his eyes he would taste the air of his youth, heavy with a war just passed, with shell-shocked nightmares and women's hands crying out for a village of lost men.

"Colvin." Dean's voice. It sounded older than he was, cut about by a lifetime of ill willings and cigarettes. "Colvin, you bastard, what is it?"

"Hello, Dean."

He would not open his eyes, would not abandon the autumn light of that long-past time when harvests were cut by hand and his hands were still scarred by school-masters' canes. Or later years, the only time his father had punched him like a man, all thought of Christian forgiveness dropped with the double provocation of a son sent down in disgrace and a published volume of licentious verse.

Colvin's hands remembered bitter herbs, iron nails. Remembered plaiting leather marked with churchyard mould.

Yesterday, a thorn had pierced his thumb right to the bone. His hands throbbed. Dean stood in the doorway, unwilling to enter, blocking the light. "I told you I weren't coming back."

"Yet here you are." Colvin's eyes snapped open to the

broken roof. The ivy, stirred by breeze, slapped its dry hands together.

"What do you want this time?"

He opened up the wickerwork of his wounded hands to show the twig of yew that nestled there, torn from above his father's grave, all smeared with his own blood.

Dean looked at it, the shape into which it had been carved. "You're mad if you think I'll help you with that."

Colvin closed his eyes again, wrapped up his carving in protecting hands.

"No," said Dean, "Not a bloody hope."

But it was time.

"Well, what the hell's it got to do with me, eh? I hear them talking in the village. You're nothing but a byword now, a bloody ghost, a revenant."

"Yet you come when I call you."

Dean coughed, a hacking sound that would kill him

before the decade was done. "And if I do? Look at you. I used to be so scared of you. But what's it ever brought you, eh? You're just a bloody gigolo, the village's prize bull with the horns to match it."

Colvin laughed, although there had been no humour in Dean's voice. "And how is Ann, your Ann? Has she worked it out yet?"

A sound of disgust in the back of Dean's throat, "Are we done?"

"No, Dean, we are not done." And it moved through him, all his years and the strength of the land, still there for him to call upon, still there to bring him to his feet, to bring from his pocket a handkerchief marked by faded blood.

Dean spread his arms and smiled like a boxer daring on the final fall. His hair was prison-short, his face edging to old age. He looked up at Colvin with a scornful hate which differed not a shade from that which Colvin had been buffeted by a hundred times. "She'll never let this lie."

"What? Even if they kill me too?"

"And how will they do that with you holed up in here like a wren in a fucking hedge?"

The chill of it went through him. "They're going to tear me hair from hair."

A laugh, "You frightened, Colvin? Can't face it like a man?"

And in the flicker of darkness as he blinked, Colvin saw the shadow of his father's face, and knew he would be able to strike the blow.

*

"You must remember, your grandmother's had a very hard life."

The engine in the car, the day bleeding out its light and the love of a book that would whisper secrets to her in lost shadows. To all this, her mother's voice was a thread that guided her back to electric clarity, to the world that claimed to be reality.

"Because grandfather is in prison?"

The sidelong look, the raised eyebrows that recalled a hundred half-ironic comments about little pitchers having big ears. "Among other things, Gwyneth. Look, she is getting on a little bit and the past, the past always looks more golden. She romanticises it but, well, I think that time in London did something to her. I think she met someone, someone dangerous."

"The Poet?"

Her mother flinched at the name. "See what I mean? The Poet. Honestly. And I don't know. She would never tell me much about it. But it wasn't all peace and love back then. It was quite seedy. Sexist, too. There were a lot of criminals, a lot of, well. She wasn't much older than you, Gwyneth, and I think she got herself very badly burnt."

An image: flames leaping out with the force of clutching hands. She shivered, not quite in fear.

"Do you know what a libertine is?"

She nodded.

"Well, that might work out very well for men, but women have to bear the price of it. That's the problem with 'Free Love'. She had me when she was very young, and she had to do a lot of it alone."

"But what about your dad?"

Already, there was a closed look upon her mother's face, and even as this frustrated her, a note sounded in her mind, calling her away to the dank spaces of the woods that lined the road, the day beyond the day, the country behind the sky.

*

A note was struck in the open space below her ribs and she answered her body's call with the same, slow certainty of the tide. Blood began its passage through her, staining her legs, a creeping kinship with the sea that called her name, the earth that turned its thoughts away from night. She left her trail upon thorn, briar, frost-sharp soil. There was a blackbird by the path, plunged into the mud, one wing raised up like the sail of a ship of bad omen. The stumps of oak lurched and mouldered, vessels broken on unfaithful sands.

The summer was gone, and with it the death-heady passion and fly-slow heat. The night was stark as the sky, as swift as a neck-snapped bird. Spring has its price.

Her bare feet defied the hardness of the ground and the blood she lost thrummed to the beat of her being. Her body was half-ghost, a moonlight thing slicked by shivers, her nipples pinched to rocks by the cold. She thought of Excalibur, the white-silver blade plunged into screaming rock, of strong grey stacks of stone battered and caressed by wind. The trees around her tutted together like spinster aunts, their long-since coppiced boles giving their years the lie. She was powerful, young, strong, and he was within her, like the circling of buzzards, like lines of verse. His spirit was her bone, his eyes within her skull. He stroked the inside of her skin and knew it for his own. Yet he stared in horror at the blood upon her thighs.

Miser.

A gulf between them, irreducible. She, open to the sky and the moon, to the wild current of the wind, lure of the sea. A binding symbiotic and complete, a price paid and received in the same moment of breath drawn. "Can you understand?" she whispered to the air in syllables that trembled through the night, that made their way in ripples back through time from this place of woodsmanship and life to find audience among graveyard branches broken in despair, to labyrinths of books and troubled dreams.

Her scarred hands smarted at the memory of midnight railing, her eyes raised to a voice half heard.

Look.

The path was blocked by a yew tree brought down by the storm. She knew, were she to strip its bark, it would be red contained by white. The needles on each tiny twig were soft as water scratching her arms, and she pulled long strands from her hair, winding them around the bitter barrier like wishing rags.

Do you understand?

The sky's rough hands had made it fall and she had left her spore without selfishness. She pulled a handful of yew, answers curling on her skin like feathered patterns of ice.

*

The sea called to him, as tight within his veins as a strand of hair pressed into wax, as the rope that he had drawn about Dean's throat.

In the night, fresh blood was black. He could taste it, as though someone had severed his tongue.

Dean kicked the air, struggled like a rabbit in a buzzard's claws, like a man caught in a lascivious embrace. Colvin looked into the face of the murdered man: white shirt spoiled by blood, scarred hands telling a path of loss and theft. Dean's cock strained his trousers, one last virility in the face of death. In Colvin's hand, a crumpled linen square stained with a fading butterfly of blood. In Dean's breast pocket there was a photograph of a girl with flowers painted on her face. In Dean's breast pocket, a photograph of Colvin himself.

Dean's heart would be straining, starved of blood and air, his brain overmastered by the blow. Three wounds, each enough to kill.

In the village, fire.

Colvin crushed the handkerchief and pressed it to Dean's side. Dean throttled slowly, turning on the rope's end. His spasms, flinches, fell away. Peace. For long moments, the sky was open above their heads, clutching this death to its breast. The night sang through his open mouth, and Colvin stood, motionless, on the roots of the gallows tree.

Then he turned and ran.

For his blood rose against him in riot, making a net, a mesh from point to point, from the sea to the village to the wood, then right up onto the moor, to King Arthur's Seat. A trap of pinpricks, snapped thorns and iron points chasing the way to memory's womb-dark space. His human life spun out behind him in all its rakish futility.

He had hoped to lay himself in the land, into their

bodies, their memories. He had left his years not in wear on his own skin, but in shadows upon their lips, their hearts. Ninety-two years stirred like an unfelt breeze, a weight of graveyard memory and stories whispered.

"Do it, or Mr Colvin will come and boil you in a pot."

"If she carries on like that, she'll be going up the hill to see Mr C."

A life of work, a stretching out of self in desperate kinship with the soil and the secrets of fertility. And what was he to them? A little thing, a small bird darting among the deepest twigs and leaves, beak hungry to snatch fragments of glory from the best efforts of better men. What was he but the King of Birds, the son of prophecy?

The sea upon the coast, black silk all capped with lace. The moon slipping into the clouds' embrace. The tide of his power turned, the Cutty Wren. Dean's death roused them from sleep, called the sleeping bead of blood in them, the memory of it on their infant mouths. The village pulled every year from him, the slow subtraction of a century.

Alys Earl

...In centrally heated homes, old women stood, old women leaned on sticks and mouthed words that their aunts and mothers had once spoken in warning or sweet memory, words that had shaped their younger lips, and with slow steps they walked towards the fire that scorched the shop-fronts in the market square...

...Mothers stirred awake beside husbands, lovers or half-empty beds. Mothers rose to the crackle and whisper of flames. Barefoot they walked, laid kisses on sleeping babies' cheeks and slipped out of doors as though towards their own infant's cries...

...Young women and girls were wrung by dreams they did or did not understand, dreams of heights and seductions won, of hot stone on bare backs and the grasping fingers of thorn trees. They rubbed hand on hand and slipped through windows, down drainpipes into the streets; even the littlest girls who slept in beds with dolls clutched to them felt the quiver of his blood in them and made their way into the night...

Scars on Sound

Your thorns...

The words, long since renounced, came crackling in his mind like branches stripped by winter, snapped by wind,

prison of my desire

caress of destruction jealous.

Your thorns promise on my skin...

Branches in the wind, swish of leaves about to fall. A clenching in the loins of sand, a sudden grip of lust. A yew tree lashed him, snatching handfuls of his hair. Its roots seized his ankle, sending him to slice his hands on stone, to think of long, round hills, of loving tongues and soft, spring rain. The cloth of the handkerchief pressed into the wound and Dean's blood passed into him.

Helpless as a child, he looked up to the stars in the night above him. Taurus bright, bore down with full fury towards the hunter, stern and implacable. From the village, solemn-wild, came a bacchante cry.

*

"I did love him, you know. Your granddad."

Nan Gower's house flickered with photographs, hand-developed, black and white, piled promiscuous: people, places, things. Also, there were shoes and books, clothes, the detritus of a thousand people's lives, all worn and touched and marked with grease. She would never say where they came from, these impressions of the unknown, these leaves slipped loose from the family albums of people Gwyneth did not know. The prints were propped on mantelpieces, loosely boxed or sometimes framed. They were smudged by umber ink of annotation, or backed with a taped lock of hair.

"I don't know why I keep all of his junk any more."

If you came upon Nan Gower unaware, she would be stroking the border of a photograph of some person she claimed not to know, running her finger along the imprint of some long-abandoned shoe. Or she would sit with her fingers in her greying hair as though, hidden in it, were something lost.

But, "I did love him, you know. Your granddad."

And Gwyneth would search sweat-fingered through the cluttered room for clues of someone she had never known. "What happened to him?"

"Don't ask your grandma that," but her mother's reprimand was so swift and without anger that she always ignored it, waiting as Nan took small sips of bright, bitter gin and her cigarette burned to a finger of ash as long and as unstable as the past.

Or sometimes, cruel in her child's curiosity, she would choose a picture she particularly liked – perhaps the pretty man with long, light hair, flared jeans and strings of beads on his bare chest – and ask, "Is this him?"

"What? No. No. Your granddad didn't care for photographs. Leastways, not ones of him."

And each of the three of them would let their eyes flicker, half furtive, to the bare spot upon the mantelpiece where Gwyneth was sure there had been a picture once.

Later, the quarrels, hushed. Her mother's voice, "He was

my father. I have a right to know." Or, "Just tell me the truth. I can handle it, if he's back inside."

And Nan Gower, "Don't bother an old woman."

"Mum, you aren't that old."

"What you don't know can't cause you pain."

Or, perhaps, "If you want to blame someone, blame the Poet."

Sometimes, when they were home again, her mother would cry, and she – ear pressed against her bedroom wall – would eavesdrop on her father's tepid comfort, and the sharp, sorrowful plaint: "If I could just be sure he wasn't dead."

But the mystery of this pressed her less hard than the books calling to her, possessive and private, so she would turn to those voices instead, letting the knowledge these others could give her fall unconsidered, cold.

*

Dawn lit candles on the oak twigs, grey light misting with an early rain that fell like dew. The earth beneath her was pitted, cigarette butts and bottle tops, bramble vines. She twined her arms into the trees, allowing them to catch her, the play of wolf-cubs before maturity, the puppy's harmless blows before instinct strikes.

In her, he recalled the feel of the land's teeth.

But to her, this timeless place unmasked. There were rabbits quiet beneath the standard oak. The other trees were many-limbed, warped by the work of man. Grinning, newborn nettles bit at her feet. The woodbine trailed and crumpled like dry straw.

The Romans had been pragmatic conquerors: lean meat and spring greens. These things made her landscape, as indigenous to her skin as the dark marks their villas left in fields, the shadows and humps that for centuries were distinct only to buzzards' eyes. And without this moulding, what would be the image of the spring? What would be the diet of poverty?

The cold nuzzled her armpits, crotch, the hollows of her neck. The fresh year and its scraped-knee cruelty, the freedom in pain. She raised her arms above her head and cried,

"Your heart heavy with rain,

Your thorns, sweet cruelty,

You, oh you, you are

The whiplash on my childhood days

The tear of wild rose on naked sides.

"And you," she whispered it to blood-stained thighs and woodland clarity, to railway scars and roads that lost their way, "you are dry words, old photographs and memories." But she lied like the land itself was a liar, shrugging off its injuries, its broken needs. "Tell me the truth, who did for you? Who took your heart?"

Gower.

"Gower was my mother's maiden name."

They never did marry.

Words waited upon her tongue, thick as the dried sand crust that lay on coastal silt, that would drag you down and drown your breath. Once, in the winter dark, he had held her as tight as the bulb holds the plant. She reached for his graveless face and knew it for her own, with all the harm he had done her.

The finest liar of them all, the landscape was dangerous. Both openly and subtly so.

Words, he whispered in her mind, *are scars on sound.*

And you were a poet once? Was that said aloud, or merely thought? There was within her a confusion, a sense of things once believed then dropped, of things inverted and cast aside like the pellet from a kestrel's beak. His ghost was thin, but powerful. He had guarded himself well, a fragment or two into the landscape, the populace: hair, semen, blood. No wonder that he had not aged like other men, that he had kept himself aloof from change.

How to explain a body captive to the moon's slow draw? The gyre of wax and wane, a frame that could bear life and swell with milk? Like the land, she covered each new wound with spring green and laughed to the watchers, *"What? This old thing?"* Her form could not have, was not permitted, his specificity.

The sky was pale, the breaking buds making it a stained-glass roof pressed down by rain. Stillness. The sense of rotting wood, of life burrowing and scrabbling close to ground. Spiders made their passage in her hair, mice peeped and scrambled through the wood. Her life flattened against this scene as she crouched naked, and she was twelve again, with birthmarked hands hearing whispers in the quiet. She was thirteen, giving her blood and name to the sea.

His memories scratched in her, too much of her. She feared to view them closely, caught by the possibility she might understand.

Above her birds of prey, called upwards by the light, lived lives of hunger and cradling wind. Buzzards lofted, mewed. Red kites were banded, russet, white and black. On the heights she had felt a kinship with them and her senses had not answered to the frantic, frightened life of things that crawled.

Scars on Sound

Winter coiled like a dragon at her heart. She had devoured it.

"Was my grandfather some kind of witch?" Her voice was not her own. It broke the promise of the spring day. The woodland started, was still.

The word comes from wickerwork. It means to bend, to weave, to manipulate.

"Wicker," she tasted the word, trying for a whisper no more foreign than the creak of trees, the sound of leaf litter collapsing upon itself. "So magic is to shape things to your need?"

But magic is a knife without a haft.

"All words are scars on sound."

Within her, a flinching, a turning away. She was unsure whose was the feeling, whose the voice.

One of them whispered, "Bastard," to the wood.

*

Colvin ran like Actaeon, unable to disown the gut reaction of the stag. The oaks snatched at him with restraining hands, the briars tripped him, brambles tasted his blood. Above, the moon winked wicked as a new-stretched bow. The flesh was stripped from his hands. He had left Dean's body on the tree.

He wept, crimson dripping from his hands, leaving a trail no hunter could ignore. The wood made angry music on his skin, the sea mocked, and Colvin shook in tremors like the fever that had sent his parents to the grave: his father first, his mother lingering behind.

The price, the way to pay for it all, all the torn feathers and kisses stolen from the marriage bed, the transit of Saturn. The wood was jealous of him, the fields too, calling for his life, chasing him back to the hanging tree where centuries of men had made their final drop, birds shot out of the sky. They cried out for him to dangle beside them, broken, a warning at the crossroads, when there had been a road there, before the coppice had tangled idle and the wild swallowed it whole.

Scars on Sound

If the village men could choose it they would drown him at the high-tide mark in a sea as salt as tears. But he would die on the hill.

Did they not know his kind could not be drowned?

But if he did not reach the hill...

His feet lost their grace. He blundered like a bull, bright in the ragged whiteness of his shirt.

*

In the field around his house, the trees rose above her head. She clambered over the wreck of the gate towards a building roots and ivy had torn down. The sea was closer than it had been the year before and there were maggots on the mess a fox had made of rabbit's corpse, fledglings crushed by the side of what had been a garden path.

That was the price paid by birds.

The house was stale with animal urine and ivy dust, rustling with the movement of feathered wings up where the roof and ceilings had given way to sky. In the centre of the floor, where long ago someone had lit a fire, were a man's shirt and trousers, folded. They were dry, old-fashioned and clean. Beneath them, a book of verse and a photograph, smudged and ruined by years of rain.

She dressed, the linen smooth against naked skin. The clothes were long, but comfortable. She found, in the trouser pocket, a twig of yew carved into the figure of a girl whose face was rubbed and worn beyond all recognition. She laughed, and caught the echo of a voice deeper than her own laughing with her.

Were she up upon King Arthur's Seat, she would be able to see across to Wales, despite the rain. As she left the house, the thorns parted to give her passage, the heather raised frail green hands in supplication. The wind was free and sharp. Moisture smoothed her face like tears.

*

An early frost. The channel clear, the Milky Way a smudge across the sky. He could leap up and fall into the sky. The starlight would pin him as sure as any spear.

Saturn winked and slipped behind the hill.

There was not a man among them.

He saw mouths, eyes he recognised, rearranged into a patchwork through the years, shot through with kestrels' brows, his own pale irises. Their flesh was cornfields to him, was the mantling sky. They were his history, his life shaped out by bodies he had touched, smiles he had kissed, and bargains he would never understand.

How could you miss that blood is not so precious to one who loses it each moon?

A shout from the woods, a sounding boom of sea on cliffs.

How could you miss the prices we pay?

So many thorns wound into his flesh, so many pins and images in wax.

The cost is death. Death of a potential, an idea.

They were no longer wild, but silent, calm.

We pay for your liberty.

They tore off his bloodied shirt, scratched his scarred skin.

He could not place the whisper in his head, rough-textured yew and sea-water from the day after a storm. Familiar as the taste of his own mouth.

It was important to recognise her call.

Hands seized him, yanking bones and kissing lips, tearing clumps of hair. Old women, lisping girls. Caught in the net of his own blood, he tripped and fell onto Arthur's Seat, bruising his thighs with a memory of childhood pain.

"And words?"

Did he whisper it? Did he speak it aloud?

Scars on sound.

Splayed, a helpless virgin before an older law. Lovers' claws, that was what they had. Bloodied, caressing claws, probing at his chest and back. They grasped his manhood like a prize, broke his fingers, stopped his mouth. And still, she whispered in his mind, as intimate as self.

Scars on Sound

It means to bend, to weave, to manipulate.

Their kisses tore his skin. They stroked and straddled him, Diana's hounds. They took his lights, his tongue, his hair. Their greedy fingers pried open joints, their tongues lapped at him. They took his bloody bones and shattered them on the rock, they wrenched apart his chest and sent him screaming into the air, into the past, into memory and myth.

Tomorrow, their minds whispered to him, *tomorrow we will remember this with shame or not at all. Tomorrow we will be washed clean and in our beds, slotting back into modern life just as one wakes from a troubled dream.*

Not he. He would brood in the landscape, hearing the sea cry out a name, hearing it whispered by a voice so like his own that it lay in shattered bones beneath the rock,

Magic is a knife without a haft.

*

A cry, or perhaps a laugh, took morning flight to the village and woke the vicar with thoughts of the girl who had come asking after Francis Colvin and vanished into the night. He rose like one who felt his age and walked from the New Rectory to the church for morning prayer.

There he saw her in the spring light, sitting by the Colvin tomb. She perched upon a newer headstone, long legs crossed at the ankle, looking with pale eyes to where a bird of prey circled the spire. As he passed her, Manishi Gower watched him but she did not speak. The words on the stone were 'Emmanuel Dean', but they meant nothing to her.

Afterword

Between the Devil and the Deep Blue Sea:

The poems of Francis Colvin are hard to find and harder to research. Had my own edition not been lost, I would perhaps investigate the copyright and find some way of making them accessible online.

Or, on reflection, perhaps I would not.

The Unquiet Grave:

An earlier draft of this story appeared on www.alysearl.blogspot in 2013.

Nunc, et in hora mortis nostrae:

As I type this, I've lived in East Anglia nearly eleven years, and have still not got used to the vastness of the horizon, the cruelty of the winter fogs. With our decaying coastlines, our fens and the great, still Broads, it seems a place where the boundaries between Earth and Sea are worn away, a place were terrible things might emerge. Local stories tell of malevolent creatures who can only be controlled by lunar light, of crimes done in isolated communities and justice exacted by vicious rules.

When the light of day is dying and the darkness comes up between the reeds like the silence between the stars, you see hares standing in the fields and hear the wind from the North Sea moaning over the broken stones of abandoned churches. Staring out at the grey water, you may feel the urge to call out, to pray, to plead, to some gentle intercessor lodged upon the moon.

Bright as Day:

This came to me, one night, as I walked the Pilgrim's Way in Kent – a thing of white chalk and tiny claws, of cold and exclusions, of childish play made terrible by the quiet of the night. It wasn't until I had children myself that I could understand what this story needed to say.

Alys Earl

Adapted to Human Encroachment:

As far as I can tell, events are portrayed as they unfolded. Names have been changed to protect the guilty and innocent alike.

Honeymoon Suite:

We are responsible for the words we say, for the monsters we let into the world. Some things, perhaps, would be better left unsaid. Sometimes what we find in our minds unsettles even ourselves – not in its base matter, but in the use to which it could be put. However, this is a collection about women haunted, about fertility and monstrous births. I feel this tale belongs here. I will not apologise for it.

Grimm's Law:

As my father and my sister's husband cleared my grandparent's house, I was struck by just how little I really knew. Spoken stories slip through your fingers, the next handful of words overwriting the previous ones forever.

Ghosts are merely what happens when you can still catch an echo of words that were spoken before.

The Song of Bill 'o Dale:

In May 1607, on the plain at Newton, men and women gathered to protest the enclosure of the Common Land by local landowners. They called themselves Levellers. During a pitched battle with a liveried militia, they 'fought desperately', but the day ended in a massacre. This story is not set in our world, but inhabits a seventeenth century with England still under the rule of embattled Plantagenet Kings. The events, however, are parallel.

The rights of, and to, the Commons are persistent themes in the history of English dissent – from the arch-poacher Robin Hood to the Inclosure Act of 1845 – and with each eruption of protest, some of that radical energy was channelled into the discussing the possibility of a fairer society. Fifty years before the events at Newton, Robert Kett (sometimes spelled Chat, or even Cat) began by protesting enclosure, and ended making demands for the manumission of bond labour.

While such rebellions agitated for the rights of the poorest in society, they were often led, begun, or at least attended by free and even landed individuals. It is easy to see the Medieval and Early Modern period as homogeneous, and governed by the strict division of class, race, gender; of the rustic and the urban; the civilised and the wild, but it is the permeability of these categories which which permits revolution and change. Kett himself was a landowner and was willing to commit treason to fight for freedom of serfs.

The folk imagination nurtures its grievances, and its memory is long.

The Maternal Line:

All the birds of all the air fell sighing and sobbing when they heard the bell toll for poor Cock Robin.

A Note on the Songs

Folk ballads form a large aspect of my storytelling. All my life I have been enchanted by their rhythms, narratives and themes. If you're curious, there are some details below.

Colvin's 'Unmarked' is similar in many ways to Keats' 'Isabella and the Pot of Basil' but my memories of the poem bring out a darker, colder tale. It seems to draw its inspiration less from *The Decameron* than from Roud 5 and 18 – ballads known as 'The Twa Corbies' and 'The Bramble Briar'.

Recorded as Roud 494, 'Who Killed Cock Robin' is a dark, and potentially ancient, nursery rhyme. It has much fallen out of popularity, for obvious reasons.

'The Unquiet Grave' is a song of mourning and loss, of the difference between life and death, and was recorded by Francis James Child as Child 78. In performance, I preface my story of the same name by singing the B version, to a tune similar to that used by The Dubliners.

The song which Gil sings is variation G of Child81, the ballad commonly known as 'Little Musgrave'. The most well-known recording of this song is on Fairport Convention's *Liege and Lief*, and is titled 'Matty Graves' – however it is more widespread in longer and less roistering versions. My favourite is that arranged by Nic Jones on his *Ballads and Songs*.

'Girls and Boys Come Out to Play' is recorded as Roud 5452 and is said to remember the children who were forced to work during the daylight hours, and who could therefore take their only recreation on the nights of the full moon. This interpretation is perhaps more comfortable than mine.

The catch in 'The Song of Bill O' Dale' is a much altered form of the Broadside ballad 'The Keeper' or 'The Hunter'. The version most people know is concerned with the poaching of deer; the original is somewhat bawdier. The changed lyrics are intended to be sung to the traditional tune. The call-and-response chorus may be elided or retained, as pleases the reader best.

Acknowledgements

First and foremost, thanks must go the Ruth Tucker for her gorgeous illustrations. Writers are egotists, and we always wish for a reader who 'gets' us – finding one who can translate that understanding into such disturbing yet beautiful images is the ultimate thrill. This book would be so much less without her work.

Secondly, to Edith, without whom there would be no book. Full stop. So now the rest of you know where to send complaints. Thank you, ninx.

Writing these stories has been a long process and there have been so many helping hands along the way. I've been blessed with the most incredible family who have been supportive at every stage of my writing career.

To my parents, who gave me the gifts of literature, literacy and the old music of these islands. I would not be where I am without ghost stories told on winter walks, and Narnia read to me over and over again. Hob — you are one of the best storytellers living, and I'll fight anyone who says different. For my first poetry gig, for teaching me how to perform, and fact checking of aeroplanes and family history, thank you. All errors are my own doing. Mumza, your support, editorial advice and alpha-reading have been given unstintingly. What's more you're the only person I'll know who'll chat for hours about medieval mystics and you've never taken me to task for walking out with your entire collection of vinyl when I left home. You're the best.

Families are not just blood, but what you make them, so to Bill and Ann, for the books, the myths, and for always taking me seriously – even if I was taking myself far to seriously. I couldn't have done this without you. Also, to Jemma Hill and Amy Harris. It's not often that the friends we make at 12 stay with us for the rest of our lives, but you were there at the beginning. I hope it was worth the wait.

Anne Hodgson – grammar goddess and proof-reader to the stars — and the supremely talented Alina Sandu deserve all the credit for making this volume look so much better than I could, and persuading me out of all the foolishness to which new writers are prone. Including ellipsies...

The Internet is a mixed blessing to writers, but my wonderful followers on Twitter – with their kind words, sense of humour, and friendship – are not mixed at all. You've educated me, chatted with me, and indulged my tendency towards stupid hashtag games. What's more, whenever stuff has really kicked off, you've been there with advice, virtual hugs and general brilliance. I spend a lot of time shut up in front of a computer screen – you taught me that the very best people can be found there. You know who you are.

All the same, thanks must go the bookselling superhero Debra Chapman for giving me a reason to drag myself out of my hermitage once a month and head down to the book group in Norwich. Also to the book-group themselves, for bringing that glorious hour of sanity. Sorry if this one isn't Claire-friendly.

To fellow writers Chris Farnell, who gave me directions through the murky world of self-publishing, and Die Booth who not only read the whole thing before any of you, but also said the words that let me know it was ready. Two stars in the firmament.

To everyone who has ever beta-d, proofed or critiqued one of these stories for me, beginning with, but not limited to Michael Gordon, Mobeena Khan, Erika Haase, Shawn Standfast, Michael Crouch, Sean Gomez, Lucy Brady, Keavy Sands, Tom Clarke and, of course, many of those named above.

Thanks in all things must go to my splendid tutors at UEA, Drs Karen Smyth, Tom Rutledge and Matthew Woodcock. I know you'd probably be appalled at me misusing my MA like this, but you taught me to ask the right questions and to suspect my own answers. What's more, you supported my passion for folklore and fable, keeping it alive and equipping me with the skills and knowledge to go for this.

This volume would have been far harder to write without the excellent resources available online, particularly www.mudcat.org and www.sacred-texts.com. Both are invaluable to anyone even remotely interested in legend and folklore, especially if all they have is a handful of half-remembered lines, or a very obscure variant. All mistakes, it goes without saying, are mine.

Last, but never least, to Mattie for love, conversation and endless tea. Every writer should have one.